SQUISHY
SHORT STORIES

ARJUN BASU

SQUISHY
SHORT STORIES

LIVRES
DC
BOOKS

Cover illustration by J. W. Stewart.
Author photograph by Jane Heller.
Book designed and typeset by Primeau & Barey, Montreal.
Edited by David McGimpsey for the Punchy Writers Series.

Library and Archives Canada Cataloguing in Publication
Basu, Arjun, 1966-
Squishy/Arjun Basu.
(Punchy prose)
ISBN 978-1-897190-37-1 (bound).
ISBN 978-1-897190-36-4 (pbk.)
I. Title. II. Series.
PS8603.A797S68 2008 C813'.6 C2008-901655-6

For our publishing activities, DC Books gratefully acknowledges the financial
support of the Canada Council for the Arts, of SODEC, and of the Government
of Canada through the Book Publishing Industry Development Program (BPIDP).

Canada Council   Conseil des Arts
for the Arts   du Canada

Société
de développement
des entreprises
culturelles
Québec

Printed and bound in Canada by Marquis Imprimeur. Interior pages printed
on 100 per cent recycled and FSC certified Silva Enviro white paper.
Distributed by Lit DistCo.

DC Books
PO Box 666, Station Saint-Laurent
Montreal, Quebec H4L 4V9
www.dcbooks.ca

For Naomi, with love.
And dim sum.

DISCLAIMER STUFF

ACKNOWLEDGEMENTS

I would like to thank:
David McGimpsey, champion, friend, hard ass
My parents for the foresight
The Charrons, my second parents
Jo and Karine, and Jaya

Milo, for being so wise and always making me laugh,
even when parenting skills call for not laughing.

CONTENTS

1 Thursday

9 The Lawn

19 Johnson's Johnson

35 Meat Man

39 Finding Something You're Good At

55 The King of Wimps

65 Two Star

79 The White Pants

83 Squishy

93 The Idols

109 Smart Men Do Dumb Things

117 The Defeated

125 Chicken Scratch

THURSDAY

Someone says, "Maybe, but not now."

Someone else says, "That means he owes you nothing."

There are men here, deep under the city, but the audible voices are all of women. There's some kind of message in that, surely, a sociological truth, except that I have yet to eat breakfast and the symbolism is lost on me.

The meaning of life only comes to those with sustenance. Didn't the Buddha figure this out? Isn't that why he's so palatable to the middle class?

Between stations, the subway's lights flicker and in that split second half of us are thinking al Qaeda and if that isn't a victory for them I don't know what is.

The train pulls into the station and bodies are exchanged. Germs move around. Jump hosts. Different strands of DNA. Constant mitosis.

The fashion changes. A pack of teenagers board, three black kids and a Latino, and you can sense everyone clutching their handbags, moving over, trying desperately to ignore them, the knowledge that their feelings are both unfair and possibly racist, but also a matter of survival. There's history in the flinch, the hesitation. Lessons learned during a long and systemic education.

The kids are well behaved despite the fact their pants start half way down their asses. I have yet to figure out the physics of these things. Nothing makes me feel older than hip hop jeans. Not even the parade of starlets on the covers of the gossip magazines, or the fact that so many magazines like that exist, or that CNN now quotes those magazines to announce their own breaking news. I once heard a story about a kid running from the cops and tripping over his own pants. There was a lesson in there for everyone but mostly for the arbiters of fashion who I have figured out don't read the papers. Ever.

The subway smells of fried foods, of a moldy type thing that in any other situation would offend as unhealthy. Body odors. Newsprint. French fries squished underfoot. The science of dirt must have a lot of interesting things to say about subway odors. The science of dirt.

This morning, in my haste to get to the doctor quickly, I neglected the following: my morning coffee; brushing my teeth; reading the sports pages; taking in the days' forecast. My ignorance of everything I need to know, combined with the fuzzy feeling coating my teeth, has rendered me numb. My ignorance is an odd shame, like your parents walking in on you and your girlfriend, naked on the floor, only because you once gave them the keys to the house, and no one ever discusses it again but it has happened and it becomes that unspoken thing that everyone remembers. Always. That's what all family conversations are: tip toeing around the unspoken. I picked up a coffee at the corner deli and it burned the roof of my mouth. I didn't dress warmly enough.

The doctor thing is nothing serious, simply a regular check-up. The joys of employment. Of a good benefits package.

When I was twelve, and still seeing a pediatrician, my mother watched as the doctor examined a stool sample, poking at my crap with a wooden stick. I can't even shit in my parents' house now for fear of my mother reliving that experience. And then telling everyone about it. There is nothing more humiliating than a stranger examining your stool. The intimacy is too much.

Another stop and an unequal exchange of bodies means the teenagers find places to sit. Each of them bops their head about to the beat in their earbuds. The train moves forward and then stops suddenly and then starts up again. Heads bob and none of them are in synch with the teenage heads. Breakfast would feel good right now. A light breakfast. Granola with yogurt. Some juice. An unhurried coffee. My morning won't really start until I get some acceptable coffee inside of me.

There is no excuse for bad coffee. Anywhere. Not in this century.

A pregnant woman takes the seat next to me. She wears dark glasses, the kind that hides either abuse or some kind of visual impairment. How do you ask someone if they are blind or not? How do you ask a perfect stranger, "what's wrong?" Or, "how did you get this way?" I mean in the real world and not on the Internet. Would the world be more civil if we could jump-start conversations without dancing our way to the inevitable questions? Civility is just another way of getting in trouble. It's when we most say what we don't mean.

Someone says, "I can't live like this anymore."

Someone else says, "Where does it say he can be this way?"

And then the train stops. It comes to a slow, gentle stop in the middle of the tunnel. I check my watch and realize something else I forgot to do this morning. I hear variations on expressions of exasperation. Now you can hear the male voices. "What the fuck?" I hear.

"Fucking hell."

"Oh, fuck."

Complaints bring out the baritones.

The train stays stopped. Shuffling. The futility of a cellphone inside a subway tunnel. The four teenagers debate the reasons for the stoppage in that loud, indifferent way teenagers have; everyone can hear their conversation. Would that teenagers were halfway eloquent.

The lights go out. And now that Al Qaeda feeling becomes something profound and palpable. As much as we don't want to admit to this, as much as we want to show the lengths of our courage, we think these things. When the slightest thing goes wrong in a public space, one of the possibilities that races through the mind is a fresh attack, a new atrocity, another unspeakable act that adds something astonishing to our vocabulary. The collective mind. One can feel that everyone else feels it. Possibility as electricity. That thought is now also what makes us New Yorkers. I imagine there are other places in the world where similar thoughts occur, similar glimpses into a very specific kind of denouement. We are not so special in this sense.

And then the lights flicker and then they are on again and then the train lurches forward and everyone loses their balance and then we pick up speed and those lurid thoughts of fires and people falling through the air and the smoke and flesh and computer parts and office stationary vanish and are replaced by smiles of relief to more than one face. Happy thoughts.

We smile when we are embarrassed and when we are frightened and when we are happy. Does that mean there is not much difference between the three? Or does that just note the social taboo against punching?

The train pulls into another station and the teenagers get off and two girls get on, each over six feet tall. They are so thin they hardly occupy the horizontal plane. They're all vertical these two. And one of them plays with her gum and says, "Can you believe it?" and the other one replies: "Assholes" to which the first one replies, "I hate them" and that's all they say.

My doctor is a Persian woman with slender fingers and a mole above her lip and a deep voice and were I more confident I would profess my love for her. She is the sexiest woman alive. I doubt very much there are too many beauty pageants taking place deep in the Islamic Republic but she is here now and could be the subject of a best selling cheesecake poster, a thought that must show my age more than my bewilderment about hip hop jeans. What do kids put up on their walls these days? Calendars?

God, I'm getting old.

When my doctor is examining me I worry about my imagination wandering off down a corridor it shouldn't go. One day, she is going to tell me I have high blood pressure and I will have to tell her I don't, it's just her touch.

Someone says, "The thing is, we don't know. We can't. That's the thing."

Someone else says, "Infinity." Or maybe she says "infinitely." It's hard to make out.

The pregnant woman is obviously not blind because she is reading a fat paperback called "Love Ever After." So now I'm thinking abuse. What kind of man would abuse a pregnant woman? Maybe her sunglasses are just the result of a change in eyeglass fashion that I have yet to notice. Or a Botox injection gone wrong. Can pregnant women take Botox? What are the ethics of that? I want to interrupt her reading. I want to ask her so many things but all of them seem inappropriate.

The thin girls are both playing with their gum. No one in the world looks dignified while playing with anything that comes out of their mouth. Girls playing with gum sport the same expression as men standing above urinals.

My doctor left Iran when she was a child. She studied at Penn and then NYU. She is just slightly younger than me. I think. She lives in Brooklyn. She is single. My god, she's beautiful.

The train pulls into a station and the pregnant woman leaves. A small man with a comb-over and the smell of exertion takes her place. The smell is on him, not his clothes, I can tell.

One of the thin girls says, "And you know what else?" She says, "They have no clue. They suck." And her friend nods vigorously and that's the end of that.

I think I should change my career. I am an accountant and it's just not fulfilling. This is my admission that I'm bored. What good is it living in New York if you're bored? It's expensive here.

I should stop being an accountant. In certain circles, it's embarrassing to admit. In certain circles, I don't talk of my profession though this is a virtual impossibility in this city. Because the second question a stranger will pose is "what do you do?" And I have to reply, "I'm a CA," and just saying this also makes me feel old. Or older than I have to be.

Travel seems an impossibility but it's what I most want. I want to be a voyager. I want to name-drop hotels and restaurants and shoe stores in far-flung cities. Perhaps I can be an accountant in various countries around the world. My firm has offices in seven countries on three continents. I should ask for a transfer. I should research the type of accountancy that will take me overseas. Perhaps to Asia. To Shanghai. I think we have an office there. To a place that is foreign enough to keep me off balance. I should do what it takes to fulfill the prerequisites that would allow me the skills to travel the world. Counting numbers. The ledger is international.

Someone says, "That's what she saw."

Someone else says, "Wow."

Next to the thin girls, an elderly man dozes off. His head falls slowly to that point where his reflexes pick it up again. I wonder what that reflex is called. What is it about the reflex that has helped us survive? How is it useful? Will he miss his stop?

Beside the sleeping man, a boy reads a *Sports Illustrated.* He is engrossed. On the cover, a muscular black man, a football player no doubt–though one I am not familiar with–hoists a smaller, though still large, man up by his pants. Without the context, and even the sub-context, the photo looks ridiculous. I only recognize a handful of players. Mostly the ones with endorsement deals. I do badly in the office fantasy pool every season.

Next to the boy, a woman keeps herself busy with a crossword puzzle. It could be *sudoku.* It's a puzzle of some sort. Its level of difficulty is hard to tell from here.

One of the girls pops a bubble. "He, like, touched you!" the other girl says. Her friend shrugs. The train comes to my stop and I get off.

I join the ranks of the commuters, the disgorged contents of an unpleasant meal. Up the stairs and out into the sunshine. My doctor's office is two blocks away. I want to love her. I want to say so much to her, and knowing that I never will does not diminish my feelings or make them sadder. I think I'm healthy. She will tell me so. I feel good. We are lucky to be living in the kind of metropolis where one rarely has to look both ways before crossing the street.

THE LAWN

Early morning. The sun rises quickly. Majestic oaks and pines and firs and maples line the street, towering over manicured lawns. Long shadows streak across the greenery, the curving road, the sidewalks. Shiny SUVs parked on driveways of the blackest asphalt. Roses. Geraniums. Evidence of pruning. Silence interrupted by birdsong.

From the northern end of the street, slowly, haltingly, a white minivan rambles its way toward its destination. The driver wouldn't know a straight line if he saw one. A kid could outwalk this minivan right now. A toddler in a Big Wheel.

The minivan struggles into a driveway, parks next to a shiny black Lexus sports coupe and stops. On the lawn, a new baseball sparkles in the sunshine. Next to the front door, a child's hockey stick, a roll of white tape hanging off its sawed-off butt end. The minivan has rolled in before the delivery of the morning paper.

Inside the minivan, Raj undoes his seatbelt and takes a deep breath. He looks into the rearview mirror and slopes down into the seat. "Fuck," he says. "Fuckin' fuck fuck."

He can smell himself. His evening is a funk that permeates his Honda Odyssey. He opens a window. And then he opens two more. His white oxford shirt is creased, stained, unbuttoned down to his navel. One foot is unburdened of its shoe. Raj wants to sleep. He wants the coming day to promise something better. He wants to erase things from his life. Starting with the night before.

A conversation from two hours ago. Raj remembers being in a bar as the sun started to make its mark on the sky. He remembers sitting around a table with three strangers. He remembers a kind of freedom that talking to strangers allows. The lack of burdens, of history, of commitments. Of promises unkept. "She saw my dick and she laughed," he said, laughing himself.

"That's awesome, dude," one of the guys said, the one with the tattoo of a woman on his shoulder. Raj was sure it was of Mother Theresa but the idea was preposterous. Who tattoos Mother Theresa anywhere?

"She fuckin' laughed at me," Raj said, grabbing one of the shot glasses on the table and downing it. Had he been drinking whiskey? Or rye? And what was the difference exactly? What is it in the process that makes them different? Or was it an ingredient? He felt he should know this.

"Well, you said you had a small dick," said another one of the guys, this one short, black, with horn-rimmed glasses. Possibly gay. "You don't advertise that. If you have that kind of problem, you wait for the makings of an erection before you show the goods."

"The truth will set you free," said the tattooed guy.

"Truth in advertising is bankruptcy," the black guy said.

At this Raj squirmed. He remembers that this line made him uncomfortable.

The third guy, tall, blond, muscular, with a black t-shirt that said *so sue me* said, "Is it really small? I mean, what are we talking about here?"

The three guys laughed. Raj downed another shot. The blond guy may also have been gay. It was possible. It was entirely possible he was in a gay bar. He hadn't noticed.

Raj shook off the shot. "I was scared," he said. "It was freezing. We were in a park. And I had to pee real bad."

"Trifecta!" yelled the tattooed guy. He picked up a shooter and the other two guys did the same and their drinks went down.

"Was your dick inside of you?" the black guy asked. "Shit."

"Scared, cold and... what was the third one?" asked the blond guy.
"He had to pee," the black guy said laughing.

Raj looks around the Odyssey. The articles of his existence. His
children's toys in the back. His wife's silver bracelet in the ashtray.
The story of his recent life is found in the crannies of this vehicle.
He does not feel remorse. He feels like he's earned something. That
he needed to get something out of his system and he did. He feels
the humiliation of his evening but not of his deeds. He smells
something fierce. Something caged. He can smell the zoo.

His wife drives the Lexus. How this happened he is still unsure,
how she ended up with the sportscar. Where was the conversation
whereby he would have to drive everywhere in a minivan? A white
Honda Odyssey? With a roof rack. With a kid's seat in the back. He
has two kids. They are terrorists. He loves them deeply. He loves
them more than his wife. He loves his wife. Just not as much as
he used to. Raj loves her like he might love a food that is good for
you, or an old sweater that is hopelessly unfashionable but that is
encoded by comfort and familiarity. That is, not at all.

His son is ten. He likes soccer and baseball and hockey. He does
well in school. He prefers cords to jeans. He laughs at Raj's jokes.
He likes hiding his sister's most beloved toys. He has a thing for
polo shirts and disdains T-shirts. What kid doesn't like T-shirts?
Raj goes on business trips and brings home T-shirts and his son
refuses to wear them. He takes them to school in his school bag
and gives them to his friends. The boy's friends wear the proof of
Raj's business travels.

Raj's daughter is seven. She wears jeans and pink dresses, often at
the same time. She flies around the house wearing pink fairy wings.
She reads Harry Potter. She reads the novelizations of movies aimed
at girls enamoured with pink as a concept. She has grown out of

her fondness of horses with wings. She also likes dancing to Raj's collection of '80s New Wave. She found "So Lonely" and sang it at tremendous volume for a week. And then she discovered "Boys on Film" and she became obsessed by Duran Duran. How was that even possible? Raj would tell the story to his friends but he's too proud to admit the Duran Duran was his. Comeback or no comeback, he's not proud of that part of his personal musical history.

Raj can see the evolution of the evening. He remembers a call for an afterwork beer. The staff was stressed and punchy. The humor was tinged with something different. Anger perhaps. Bile. The sarcasm was cutting, close, not so sarcastic in the analysis. A junior account manager kept affecting an Apu style Indian accent everytime Raj handed him more work. He went around the office saying, "Raj has given me yet another task. I won't be making him a Squishee." Colleagues would write bitchy emails and end them with a smiley emoticon. Raj hated that symbol, the easy way out it provided. He hated what that emoticon promised, or didn't promise, its shorthand. He was young enough to appreciate the efficiencies of email but old enough to bemoan what it had done to inter-office communication in particular and to the art of correspondence in general.

Five of them went across the street for beers. Popcorn. Darts. The possibility of karaoke. Raj had always thought darts and karaoke were a dangerous, perhaps even fatal, mix; though he'd never heard of anyone getting hurt from singing "Summer Loving." Beers and laughter and the knowledge that the account was as good as theirs. Advertising people being smart and hip. Or at least being good at acting smart and hip. Double entendres and puns and one-liners and put-downs. And darts. Raj was good at darts.

And then Raj stood up and walked over to the karaoke machine and sang "Kashmir." Ironically. He did the Robert Plant wail with such over-the-top attitude he almost threw up. He struck the right pose. His air guitar caused shrieks of approval. Laughter. Spontaneous applause.

He unbuttoned his shirt down to the navel. He looks down at his shirt and wonders if it's been unbuttoned all night.

He creates advertising. He is Creative Director at a boutique agency. He has created advertising for puppy food, for adult diapers, for pizza sauce, for garage door openers. Last year, his print ads for fruit-flavored condoms won international awards. He has created ads for a line of discount basketball shoes. For a heartburn remedy. For a high-end home theatre. For white paint.

For Raj, advertising is the most important industry in the world, the linchpin to the global economy. Without advertising, no one sells anything and no one buys anything. Without it, there is no need, no desire. He sees it as not just necessary but an artistic and noble line of work. It is the beginning of the chain of consumption that feeds millions, that clothes and houses. His wife sees it as manipulative and a cop-out for true artists. The world was more creative before artists became advertisers, she says. She is a family doctor. Raj can never argue the nobility of his work with her. He loses before he opens his mouth. When an argument, about anything, gets especially heated, she might say, "I saved a child's life today. And you?"

Raj makes four times more money than his wife does. She doesn't care. But it's always in the back of his mind. This fact. It's not important, he says, but he knows he's lying. His earnings make him feel big. Bigger. Not just a grown-up, but a provider. A success. The travails of work are long forgotten by the time he slaps down the plastic to pay for something else. Something new. By the smiles on his children's faces when he has provided them with another kind of happiness. By the fact that he bought both the Lexus and the stupid minivan.

Raj threatened to sing again. And again. He knows he's drunk when he suggests he sing "Rio."

"You're uncouth," the head writer said, throwing popcorn at Raj.

"Fuck that," Raj said. "I'm honest, that's all. You can't handle the truth!"

Laughter.

"The truth is this," said Raj's assistant. "Personality wins. Game over." Sexy, smart, decisive. How often had Raj lost himself in her being? And her breasts.

"You're an elitist," said the head writer.

"You're an elitist who loves people," said the assistant.

"That combo can and should get you shot," said the writer. "Or at least wounded."

"I'm going up there," Raj said, getting up.

"Oh, please," said the assistant.

"Sing something fun for once," said a junior copywriter, the chunky girl who wore vintage dresses in various shades of brown.

"I'm going to bring this shit down," Raj said.

"Oh fuck, he's going to sing 'Kashmir' again," the writer said. And he does, in a fashion. He sings "Kashmir" over the tune of "Yellow Submarine."

There are grass stains on the shirt. How is he going to explain grass stains? And the shoe? Where could the shoe be? Three hundred dollar Pradas. And for what? He opens the cool box by the glove compartment and takes out a bottle of water. He doesn't drink it. He imagines himself floating, somehow, above the house, watching it, the knowledge of his family inside, the silence of the place. He imagines a long, endless shower. Where was his shoe?

He left his colleagues at the bar and walked down the street to grab a hot dog. He ate two. And while eating he was drawn into another bar, one that he had never entered, and he sat himself at the bar, and he ordered a beer. A long narrow room, a neighbour- hood joint with an old jukebox dominated by heavy metal classics. Like "Kashmir." He finished the beer and as "Hell's Bells" started their chime, he ordered another. He doesn't really remember any more. He can make out the pool table in the corner, empty, the green felt worn down by years of drunken, aggressive play. He can picture the group of college kids in the corner downing shots and high-fiving each other and talking in that loud way drunken college guys talk. He remembers a girl at the end of the bar but he can't remember her face. At one point he said, "I don't want my kids slinging burgers when they get older," but he can't remember the context of this or who he said it to.

Raj takes a swig of water. He holds the bottle to his forehead. He looks at the baseball on the lawn, his son's baseball. He takes another swig of water. He holds the water in his mouth, his cheeks distended, a squirrel hoarding nuts.

There was a park. At some point he ended up in a park. With that girl. Or maybe another one. A black lace push up bra. He can see that. But he was in a park and then he pulled down his pants and the girl had laughed. He felt terror and shame and he ran to the bushes and peed. And then he decided he had to get home and he left the girl in the park, alone with her laughter.

He couldn't find the Odyssey. He couldn't find his way back to the office. He walked into a bar and had shots with three guys who were possibly gay. And then, amazingly, he found the office. The sky was going from deep purple to azure. He got in the minivan, drank a bottle of water, and decided to drive home. With the fuzzy knowledge that he hadn't really done anything wrong finally. Sort of. He had exposed himself to a stranger. But all that got him was humiliation. The makings of a secret. Of mythology.

Raj opens the door. A portly middle-aged man wearing a red shirt and two sizes too tight running shorts jogs past. Raj eyes him suspiciously. This is not a man he recognizes from the neighbourhood. He has opened the door but he doesn't exit. He doesn't know his next move. Does he go inside and head straight for the shower? Does he make himself breakfast? Does he crawl on the lawn and roll around? Does he get back in the minivan and ram it into the garage door? Does he drive the stupid thing out of the driveway and keep going until it runs out of gas? Raj wants to cry and he doesn't want to cry. He'd rather the purity of an extended amnesia.

The drive home was slow, deliberate. He turned a fifteen minute drive into one lasting over an hour. There were times when he thought being pulled over by cops would be a great way to explain the night away to his wife. Except for the time. He could never explain being pulled over so early in the morning. It was better to get home. To lie on the couch in the living room and contemplate the universe. He needed the comfort of home. Its safety.

Raj puts a foot to asphalt. And then his bare foot touches down. The ground is cold, not yet radiating the sun's warmth. He puts the keys in his pant pocket. His knees are grass stained as well.

He was on his knees at some point, he realizes. He walks to the baseball and picks it up and examines it. The ball is new. There's not a scuff mark on it. He imagines throwing the ball through the bedroom window and running away, hoping that his children are right behind.

JOHNSON'S JOHNSON

This all starts with a baseball card. That one threshold of success, the baseball version of the bar mitzvah, the object after which a ball player can be called major league. Johnson's baseball card had a flaw. Flaw is a good word for it. Mistake is too harsh and, given what happened, perhaps too cruel.

Johnson was a good kid. The kind of boy that adolescent girls' mothers found safe, unthreatening. Acceptable. An unspectacular boy growing up in Peru, Illinois, Terry Johnson had one gift, the kind of gift that unspectacular boys across America aspire to in the hopes of lifting them out of their unspectactularness or their future jobs at tractor dealerships, or small offices with yellow fluorescent lighting where the crude interpersonal politics play out with all the predictability of the group hug in a sitcom stuck in a bad time slot.

He played baseball. The sports editor at the local paper called him The Inca. An all-round player who could field and hit, possessed of a golden arm, an accurate throw, lightning quick reflexes, a heavy bat. Size 12 feet. The size of his feet were public knowledge, for reasons unfathomable to him, like the price of hog futures.

The spectacular kids in this part of Illinois all go on to play football or basketball. The unspectacular ones play baseball. And Johnson's talents shone like a magical light over all the unspectacular kids.

He got drafted out of high school by the Chicago Cubs. In Peru, they celebrated with a "Terry Johnson Day," consisting of a parade, a fried chicken dinner in the middle of town, and speeches by the mayor, his coach, various local business leaders, the president of the PTA and the reigning North-Central Illinois Corn Queen. Johnson received a key to the city from the chamber of commerce. Townspeople figured his future was assured. That he got drafted by the home team was simply God working His wonders.

Johnson reported for Rookie League duty with the team in Mesa, a town he found hot and strange. He settled in at third base, drew the attention of the Cubs' scouts with his stellar defensive play–only four errors!–and before the season was out was up in Boise. In the off-season, he returned to Arizona to play winter ball and concentrate on his hitting and in the spring was asked to report to the AA team in Jackson, TN. And then he broke the wrist on his throwing hand fielding a bunt and lost a season.

Fortunately for him, he was in the Chicago Cubs system. As his coach in Jackson said: "Son, the Cubs have perfected the art of finding new ways to suck. You're a good third baseman. You'll be in the Show soon enough. Just keep working."

He rehabbed in Chicago, attended games at Wrigley, breathed in the air of major league baseball with visions of glory–he could see his face on billboards, he could imagine the endorsements for deodorant, for Mexican restaurants, for local car dealerships. The team put him up in a luxury hotel just off the Magnificent Mile. He delighted in being able to order up cheeseburgers, through room service. He drank all the soda from the minibar and when he built up the nerve, he drank the beer, too. His dad came up to Chicago and Johnson gave him a tour of the innards of Wrigley: the clubhouse, the weight room, the dugout. His dad was impressed. And proud. Johnson was the happiest son in the world.

He returned to Jackson and finished the season strongly, hitting .323. The next winter, he was told he would be attending the Cubs' spring training camp in Mesa. He signed a new contract for money his agent called, "Serious, honey."

He bought his dad a lightning blue Dodge Durango and his mother a set of high-end garden shears housed in a soft, burnished leather sheath. She called all her friends to spread the news. The garden shears were the source of much envy among the ladies of Peru.

The first two days of camp went by like a runaway train. The condiments on the buffet table were proof of the elevated station of his life. "Just wait until the regulars get here," a training room guy said. "You're going to see some sweet, sweet food on that table. You don't serve a millionaire a peanut butter sandwich."

"What's wrong with a peanut butter sandwich?" asked Johnson.

"You don't eat peanut butter, when you can eat steak," the training room guy said. "Unless you're Elvis."

The following week, with camp in full swing, Terry Johnson had photographs taken by six different baseball card companies. He was thrilled. He felt, finally, as if he belonged. He called his father and they marvelled at the path Johnson's life had taken and how far he had come. He was only 21. He had just earned the right to drink in every state.

He did not notice the flaw in one of the cards. It was too obscure. It was only there if you looked hard enough. And if you knew where to look.

Johnson was cut from camp and assigned to AAA Des Moines. One step from the bigs, close enough to home that his parents could take in his play, he could taste his coming achievement. Des Moines was like Peru but a lot bigger and with more Mexicans. And then the Cubs pulled off one of those blockbuster trades that make headlines for weeks and burn up phone lines and cause a lot of shouting and consternation in the media, and out of it they found themselves with one of the games' best third basemen. Johnson read the news and called up his agent. "What does it mean for me?" he asked.

"It's not good, I'm going to be honest," his agent said.

"I want to play for the Cubs. They're my team," Johnson said.

"I know. But I'm going to be honest, honey, this isn't good for you."

"I'm third on the depth chart now."

"At least," the agent said.

Johnson spent the next two weeks tearing up the Pacific Coast League. He hit north of .400, with highlight reel plays in the field. His play made him impossible to ignore. He was named the league's player of the week. Pete Gammons mentioned his name on TV. A week later, in early July, the Cubs lost two players on the same play, a clumsy play worthy of every sports blooper show in the world if only the thing hadn't hurt the two players so much. An out of reach game. The Cubs in the field playing their second string. And the back-up third baseman goes running after a pop up in foul territory, he goes after it hard, perhaps too hard, perhaps because he knows he needs to live the cliché and really put in 110% every time he gets on the field, what with the blockbuster trade and all, and he leaps for the ball, barrelling into the dugout, his cleats carving a sinister-shaped gash into the chest of the all-star third baseman. The third basemen goes head first into the concrete floor of the dugout. Mayhem ensues. And Johnson gets called up just before the Cubs are set to embark on a road trip. With stops in Milwaukee, Denver and Phoenix.

And this is when the flaw in the card was discovered. A collector in Chicago examines Johnson's card. Johnson is leaning forward, his glove at the ready, awaiting the next screamer. He looks like a cheetah stalking antelope. He is serious, professional. Expectant. In his eyes, the confidence and ambition of someone who truly believes he is a major leaguer, someone who sees in this very photo the beginning of a life fulfilled. A life foretold. There is a hole in his pants. In the crotch. And out of this hole, something. Let's just say this: Johnson did not wear his jock strap that morning. They were only taking pictures after all. He would not need it. At least that was his thinking. It was a rookie mistake. No one had told him this kind of thing was even a possibility. And while that something peering out of the hole is not all that clear, there can be no doubt as to what it is. The shape is too familiar. And the collector knows he has something lucrative and funny and all too perfect. He knows it has the potential to be big. "I just have to play my cards right," he thinks.

The collector posts the news on his website. He would have a website. Everyone picks it up. A small story at the end of SportCenter. Letterman jokes about it. An indie band in Milwaukee renames themselves Johnson's Johnson. They immediately book themselves on a month long tour of the upper Midwest. They record a cover of "Norwegian Wood." And then, just for fun, "Black Hole Sun." The press they receive is like the sudden downpour that precedes a hurricane. They get an entourage that consists of more than girlfriends and family. They start using the word "big." The band's story is, simply, a message about the power of branding.

Johnson's father calls him and tells him not to worry about it. This is just one of those things; it will blow over. He's a ball player, not a model.

"What does being a model have to do with my card?" Johnson asks.

"You know what I mean, son," his father says.

"I don't."

"You do."

Johnson thinks about his father's words, about the possible meaning of them. "No," he says. "I don't."

Silence on the other end. "You do."

Johnson hears no end to the ribbing once he enters the Wrigley Field clubhouse. The pitching coach calls him Johnson Squared, which goes above Johnson's head and keeps sailing, all the way to Waveland Avenue. Johnson gets his locker. And then is told to pack up. He is given coordinates and told to report back to Wrigley Field in four hours for the drive up to Milwaukee. He is given the standard rookie orientation kit. The manager comes over and sits down next to him, welcomes him to the big leagues, and tells him he is here for as long as he deserves it, that his play will determine when and if he is sent down, not the players on the injury list. Only he could lose his spot on the roster. The manager says he's studied the tapes and considers him an upgrade in the field. "Let's get to work, son," he says, patting his back. "Just go out and show everyone what you can do." He pauses and stares into Johnson's eyes. "You're going to get a lot of advice and that's all fine but this is my team so my advice is the most important. I've been around this game a long time and I've learned things." He pauses again, for effect, and Johnson makes a mental note, prepared to take in the most important words of his life. "This is what I've learned: Sometimes, you gotta scratch," the manager says. "And sometimes you just need to adjust." He pats Johnson's back again and gets up. "This is your time, son," he says before walking off.

Johnson returns to his hotel room and packs. He feels disappointed by the denouement that is Milwaukee. He's been there too often and he's eaten all the good sausages he cares to. He's finally in the big leagues and he's playing in a city he's been to dozens of times. He's never been to New York. To LA. He's never sat in first class on an airplane.

His family will drive up. At least there's that.

The bus ride is a long game of poker. Johnson was told before the first hand that he should never win, it's a right a rookie has yet to earn and so when he draws a flush, he puts his cards down and folds. In this way, the drive costs him two hundred dollars; the cavalier way in which big leaguers play with money feels wrong to the son of a tractor salesman from Peru, Illinois.

The team checks into their hotel and most of the players nap. Johnson can't. He stares out the window of the hotel, marvels at the idea of making the Show, of being in the Show, of being a part of the Show. He stretches and stretches some more. He showers. He calls his father, staying at a Motel 6 near Miller Park. "I'm nervous," he admits. "I can't believe this is happening."

"It's all you've ever wanted," his father says.

"I'm going to puke," Johnson says.

And he does.

Later, a bus takes the team to the ballpark, a structure that hovers before them like a giant hangar. The bus enters the bowels of the thing and the team walks past a phalanx of photographers and into the locker room to suit up and take batting practice. Johnson walks to the dugout and then out onto the field and is... underwhelmed. A threat of rain means the roof is closed. The eerie quiet of a city during snow. "It's not much," says the starting second baseman, a fleet-footed black kid from Miami just two years Johnson's senior who won over two thousand dollars on the drive up. "It's boring. It's got no personality."

Johnson checks the line up card; he's batting sixth. In the first inning, the Cubs load the bases on three walks. The clean-up hitter strikes out. Johnson saunters over to the on deck circle. With the Brewers suffering through their usual dismal season, the crowd is no more than 10,000. Maybe eight. He hears a man selling popcorn. He hears cries of "Beer!" and "Over here!" and "Make that four!" In the fifth spot, the centre fielder, a bruising Dominican named Hector, strafes one into left field scoring two. Johnson steps up to the plate. He takes the scene in and hears a mother tell her daughter she can't have any ice cream. "I brought carrots for you," the mother says. Johnson feels ripped-off somehow. He's played in front of more people in Des Moines. He hates that he's in Milwaukee. He gets angry. "Is this all there is?" he asks himself. And he strikes out on three pitches.

In the fourth inning, he throws a routine grounder into the Brewers' dugout.

In the fifth, he notices a chesty blond in a tight white t-shirt holding up a sign in the empty seats down the right field foul line. It says: Show us your johnson, Johnson!

In the eighth, he drops a pop fly.

Later, at a strip club, watching a stage with fifty naked women, one hundred breasts, undulating to the stoner horniness of Snoop Dogg, Johnson downs a beer and yells "Fuck!" No one hears him. The vast fields of nudity, the endlesness of it, the Amazonian expanse of Amazons, it must be noted, did nothing to his johnson.

He is benched for the second game.

In the third game, Johnson rips one into the left field corner. The first base coach waves him on. Johnson rounds first and feels a pop. He kind of hears it. A pop. It is the sound of a bat not quite connecting on a fastball. Before he even hits the ground, he knows he has done something very, very bad. Something violent has happened within him. He tries to crawl to first base. He has the presence of mind to try. But the first baseman tags him out. "Sorry, man," he says.

At the hospital, Johnson is attended to by a nurse that he thinks should come with wings. She holds his hand as the doctor examines his groin. She strokes his hair as the reality of a severely damaged groin hits Johnson with the force of a twister. He sees the end of his career. She says, "No."

"I'm finished," he says. "I'm done. I'm going to go home and sell tractors," he says. "I'm going to be a tractor salesman."

"Don't give up," she says.

"It hurts so much," he says, pleading.

Johnson returns to Chicago in despair. And as he sinks into a kind of stoic depression he hears the nurse's sweet voice, her words. She helped him and he feels he owes her something. He undergoes surgery. And then he hits rehab with a *Rocky*-like determination.

Her name is Linda. The nurse. The nurse's name is Linda. Johnson was so pathetic, so desperate, his fatalism so profound, she gave him her email address. And now Johnson decides to use it. And they start flirting on line. And Johnson learns first hand how dirty a word can be. And what kind of turn-on a turn of phrase can be. And the intimacy that can develop between two people miles apart just because one of them loads each and every word with innuendo. With meaning. Where even the word "nurse" is typed with the promise of something bigger, more profound. More dirty.

The groin is going nowhere. Johnson was right to feel so pessimistic the night of the tear. The muscles had left the bone. The doctor had used the term "loose groin." He had said, "It's like your waist fell off." Two months later, and Johnson's groin is stiff and unpleasant feeling. It is not doing its job. He's lost mobility. His gait is a kind of shuffle. The team doctor says this is going to take at least six months. Longer perhaps. Johnson asks Linda to come down to Chicago. She does. After she leaves two days later, she still can't say she has seen anything in the city. Johnson is pretty sure he is going to marry her.

He tells her he loves her. "You're just saying that," she says.

It's true, he says.

"I love you, too," she says. And with that she gets in her car and drives off and is gone.

Standing there, watching her leave, he takes out his cellphone and calls his father. "I met the girl I'm going to marry," he says.

"The nurse?" the father asks.

"I'm in love."

"I'm happy for you, son."

"She's it."

"That's good, son," the father says. "If she's a nurse, she's a good person."

"She is."

"And the groin?"

And with this question, Johnson breaks down.

When Johnson was three years old, he told his first joke: He danced around the kitchen singing, "Poo poo Peru." He repeated this like a koan until his mother banished him to his room. For some reason, Johnson hears this during rehab. When the old Hispanic physiotherapist is stretching his groin in ways it does not want to go, he hears, "Poo poo Peru."

Rehab goes nowhere. It leads to Peru. To Johnson on his parents' couch, red and orange, twenty years old, threadbare, a couch that has witnessed things Johnson would be ashamed to admit to his mother. Out for a walk, exploring childhood haunts, Johnson comes across the old ball field. Above it, Old Glory flutters against an ocean blue sky. Johnson has heard that flag crackling in the stiff Midwestern breeze since his childhood. This is his field, and it feels like a postcard from another era. It is where Johnson lived out his dreams of youth. It is where he stopped being unspectacular. He sees the field and he feels young. And he tries to run toward it. He wants to jog to the flagpole and touch it. And he realizes he can't. He can't even push himself into a trot. He is incapable of anything more than a spirited walk. He could not run away from a small, lame dog.

He returns to his parents' home. He calls Linda. "I have to quit," he says. "I can't do it. I can hardly walk. This isn't going to work."

Linda listens to him and listens to him cry and she feels what he feels and understands the helplessness of being miles away when the man you love is pissing on his dream, is admitting the end of a life and she knows she wants to be there when he starts his life anew. "I'm coming," she says. "I'm coming to Peru."

Johnson's Johnson releases an album that all the critics notice. Relegated to a college favorite on campuses across the Upper Midwest, the band is suddenly national. They feel this. They are booked nationally. They play *Jimmy Kimmel.* In England, the *NME,* in its usual extravagant manner, calls them "The most magnificent American band playing right now." They play New York's Mercury Lounge for four nights. They play Austin City Limits. The album, called Squibbler, cements their status in the country's indie rock firmament. On the back of the CD, amidst a collage designed by the lead singer's girlfriend, is the baseball card, a sly reference to the origins of the band's name.

With Linda by his side, Johnson announces his retirement to three reporters and family and friends, and a representative from his agents' office, in the gym of his old high school in Peru. His agent calls in a favour and gets him a meeting with a sports talk station in Chicago. Big Jim McNeil, "The loudest mouth in Chicago" is a fan of Johnson's Johnson. He noticed the name of the CD and gave them a shot. And he thinks it would "fit" to have the real Johnson on the show as part of his "Den." Before the interview, Johnson stops by a quiet bar for a beer. Which becomes three. Which becomes a rumination on the sorry arc of his career, on the anger he feels toward Milwaukee, on the nature of dreams. On the fickleness of fate. "You sound like a friggin' asshole," the bartender says.

Despite the alcohol, or perhaps because of it, Johnson slays during the interview. Big Jim sees in Johnson a kindred spirit, a Midwestern kid worthy of something more than what life has dealt him. Someone broken down but not entirely broken. Big Jim sees in Johnson something that he knows will connect with the listeners of this city. Johnson starts in two weeks.

Later that evening, enjoying a steak with Linda, he asks her to marry him. "You've been drinking," she tells him.

"Doesn't matter," he says. "I could be drinking milk. I've wanted to marry you forever. I know it's true. You're for me."

He doesn't have a ring. And so next day he buys one. And he asks her again. This time in front of Wrigley Field. And this time he has a ring for her. And this time she says yes.

They buy a house in Oak Park. Linda finds a job in a hospital in Palatine. Johnson buys a red Mustang. He starts work. And his riff, for whatever reason, becomes centred on his visceral hatred for Milwaukee. At least once a show, he lets go with some bile. Helped, no doubt, by his pre-show drink. Big Jim calls Milwaukee "Johnson's Waterloo." A sample riff: "I had major league dreams. I was a little kid from a little town in Illinois and I played ball for the Cubbies and I could have lived the American dream but I got called up to the Majors to play in a two-bit stadium in a two bit town where they have more sausage than people and I tore the hell out of my groin and that was all she wrote. These folk have races with sausages, people! What does that say about the men of Milwaukee? I'm asking. A bunch of cheeseheads cheering on a bunch of overgrown sausages! There was loser written all over this thing. From the start. Loser! I was a major league loser. And that was that. The most big league thing I ever did was go to a strip club and lose two hundred bucks playing poker on a god damned bus. I never even got to sit in first class! My only road trip and I rode a bus! I was a Cub and I never played at Wrigley! And now I'm on a stupid radio show. I'm a loser!"

The audience loves it. During his riffs, which can come on at any time, Big Jim can be heard guffawing. You can almost see his belly hopping up and down. His big belly. In Chicago, a name like Big Jim is almost redundant.

Johnson is an angry man. There is no doubt about it. And his anger is somehow paying off. He represents everyone who ever thought they could somehow make it if only things weren't so stacked against them. He's playing to the bleachers. He knows it.

He drinks. When Linda announces her pregnancy, Johnson is already pickled. He's had six double bourbons after work. He slobbers kisses on her and she recoils. "Is that how it's going to be?" she asks. "You're going to be a father and you do nothing but drink."

"I'm a radio star," he slurs.

"Your act is all about how angry you are! You're playing a character. And then you bring that guy home!" She feels alone in this city. She works hard. The city is too big for her. She hates his drinking. She feels helpless to do anything about it. And now they're going to start a family.

That weekend, in Peru, Johnson and Linda announce the pregnancy. Johnson's parents cry tears of joy. Johnson's father pulls out stale cigars. Johnson's mother takes Linda aside and takes her to Johnson's old bedroom. The shelf is festooned with his baseball trophies. They glimmer. Johnson's mother still dusts in here. She hands Linda a pair of baby shoes and a blanket. "These were Terry's," she says.

"Mom, I'm worried about him," Linda says. "He's drinking too much."

Linda contacts the major league players' union and they recommend a counselor not far from their house. Johnson is incensed. The insinuation is, to him, nothing more than a show of a deep and abiding disloyalty. He does not think he needs help. He storms out.

On the next show: "I hate Milwaukee. I hate that place. That place has good brats and good beer and that's it. The beer is awesome. And custard. They're proud of their custard. What kind of a place is proud of custard? And the strippers aren't bad. You should see them! Fifty on stage at once. Naked! That's one hundred headlights shaking in your face! Otherwise, nothing good has ever come out of that place. I hate it. This is how twisted the place is, people: Their criminals eat people. The place breeds cannibals! It's probably the custard! Nothing good ever came out of that place. Except beer. And Harleys. I went to Milwaukee and all I got out of it was a wife!" Big Jim likes that line a lot.

Linda doesn't. "You need help," she tells him.

"I don't want to hear it."

"I'm not bringing a child into this kind of house," she says.

"Do what you have to do," he sneers.

And she does. The next day, she's gone by the time he's home from work. He only finds the note the next morning. He calls in sick to work. He drinks until he passes out, on the dining room table. He pisses his pants and he doesn't care. He calls the station later that day and delivers a drunken rant that has Jim trying to cut him off. When Johnson starts screaming, "I love you Big Jim! You're my family!" Big Jim has the good sense to hang up.

The next day, Johnson calls the counsellor.

He puts the house on the market. Linda sends a letter telling him that she has a lawyer and will be writing up divorce papers. She concedes that she gave up early. She doesn't apologize for it, however. She says she's keeping the baby. They can work that out later.

Johnson buys a condo in Wrigleyville. He didn't set out to. It just happened. He buys a loft, big, airy, bright. He's going to be an urban bachelor. From out of the windows in the corner, he can make out the lights of Wrigley Field. He starts to eat a lot of burritos. He joins a gym. The radio show is the number one rated sports talk show in the city. He attains a level of celebrity that feels right to him. A kind of middle class of fame. He feels he's where he deserves to be.

On this Saturday, he decides to take in a ball game at Wrigley. The sun is warm, the sky hazy with the summer's heat. Baseball weather. He heads out on the twenty minute walk and comes across a garage sale. He peruses the racks, the books on sale, the CDs. He finds a CD by Johnson's Johnson. Their latest, Ballpark Franks. On the back, the baseball card. He stares at it, at the hole. The fault. The thing. What would life have been like if he'd just worn his jock strap that morning? Johnson buys it for five dollars. And then he places it on the street. He watches the traffic roll over it. He sees the case crack and the CD fly through the air. A city bus comes by and crunches the CD and Johnson smiles. He watches the traffic kill the thing. He watches as the traffic stomps it until it is nothing but dust.

MEAT MAN

I don't know what the hell she sees in him. I have no idea what it is about him that makes him more attractive than me. It can't be a money thing because I have more of it, I'm sure, unless there's some hidden family thing I don't know about. My house is bigger. My car is nicer and I wear better clothes. Maybe I spend too much on clothes, well shoes, but it's a weakness I *acknowledge,* like my other weaknesses, there's no hiding anything with me. Maybe it's a weakness to be so honest about everything, to admit, over the phone, yes, I ate some bad chicken and my stomach's a bit upset, or that I'm not going to your parents because I'm going to the game but, c'mon, they were awesome seats, so what, honesty is a good thing, at least that's what everyone says. Or is honesty like chewable vitamins, good for you but bad tasting? I mean, why can't someone make a tasty chewable vitamin? If we can send a picture-taking rover to Mars, why can't we make a vitamin that doesn't taste like chalk?

I admit faults and always have, I was *open* with her but I'm not a hundred percent transparent. What the hell is transparency anyway? How the hell can anyone be transparent? Everything is too layered for that kind of thing. Why does everyone want black and white when everything is a shade of grey? I mean, I have absolutely *no* idea what she sees in him that she doesn't see in me. This is what I'm getting at.

I gave up hot dogs for her. When we started going out she said I couldn't eat anything *processed.* So I said, fine, I'll eat organic. I'll get to know the god-damned name of the god-damned pig before I eat the god-damned ribs. I gave up a lot for her is what I'm saying.

Worse, and this makes this thing sting like a hundred wasps descending on my naked sugar-coated body, worse, he's my friend. Was my friend. And she goes and leaves and says, "He makes me so much happier than you ever could." I don't even *get* that. She's comparing apples and oranges. What the hell kind of comparison is that? And what in god's name is she so unhappy about? She's got everything she needs in this world and OK, she wanted kids, and I wanted to wait and I didn't really think our relationship was that far along, but she's starting over with this guy and unless he wants to drop everything and have kids right now, she's taken some steps back, at least as far as I'm concerned. Is he secreting some kind of kid friendly hormone that I don't have? This is what I'm asking, if there's an issue, it's the kid issue because I did not give her any other reason to dump me suddenly in the middle of a freakin' goat cheese pizza and tell me that she was moving in with Carl.

I should have asked some questions. Like, how long had she been seeing him. Meaning what was the level of the deception because surely there was some kind of behind-my-back thing going on. Motel rooms and secret emails and *gifts*. Talk about not being transparent. And another thing: why? What did I do, was there a moment, did I do something wrong that I was unaware of, was there something I could have done differently, all of these things, I could have asked? I would have *changed* the defects she was perceiving–no question about it. I already ditched the processed meats and the soft drinks and the Doritos. And she couldn't see my commitment to the relationship? My love?

I do not believe she faked a single orgasm and I made her come every time. This is the honest truth. I don't understand what she sees in him. Frankly, he's not even that good looking and he's going bald and he's got small hands if you know what I'm getting at and he dresses funny. I'm a much better dresser, I said that already. Plus,

I jog. I'm in shape. That means I have stamina. I'm a good-looking guy, listen, I'm good-looking and I have a nice personality and I like *giving* presents, I *enjoy* giving presents, other people's happiness makes me happy. I'm a giver, not a taker.

I bet Carl can't even balance his check book.

I don't know, I don't know, I don't know what the hell she sees in him. She took her two pieces of furniture from my place and I can't replace them. Replacing them would be like admitting to all of this and I can't do that. It would mean moving on and I'm not ready to move on, not when my girlfriend left me for one of my *friends*.

She took a recliner, which, to be honest, I hated, it was ugly but comfortable as hell. I loved watching football from that recliner, I loved snuggling with her on the recliner while we watched some chick flick on the DVD–oh, she was big into the kind of stupid movie that has her crying by the end–so yes, it was ugly but I had good memories on that recliner and so what it if didn't go with the rest of my furniture, which is definitely more contemporary, I love that word, but the important thing is I loved her and she loved the recliner and that was all that mattered to me. I'm a *giver.* The second thing she took was a corner table, which, again, was ugly but kind of key to the living room in that all of our photos were on it. And a few plants. And now the photos are on the floor and so is the plant and, OK, the plant looks fine, but the photos are going to have to go especially since they are of *us* and now I have to ask myself, what the hell happened? And where the fuck am I supposed to sit while watching football?

I'm not so stupid, I believe that: I believe I've had to use my smarts to get what's come to me and then I get blindsided by something this big it makes you question everything, it tears a hole out of you so big that you have no idea where the hell anything is going and the color of the world changes and up becomes down and the laws of physics shift completely and you look at yourself in the mirror and you don't recognize anything you see. What kind of a person just walks out on you? That's what I want to know.

Before we started going out, she said, "Are you a Meat Man?"

And I said, "What does that mean?"

And she said, "I'm a vegetarian and I don't appreciate people who eat meat."

And I admitted I was a Meat Man as she put it.

And as she laid out the ground rules I asked if I could eat a hot dog at a baseball game, for example, because a ball game with, what, sushi, doesn't work for me, I'm not nibbling on carrots at a ball game, I'm just asking, and she said, "If you want this to work."

And I said fine. I said, "I'll abstain from whatever it is you find distasteful." I said that, exactly that way.

And I'm wondering. Should I throw the photos out or just put them in a drawer somewhere? Because maybe some day she figures things out and comes back to me. This is what I'm thinking.

FINDING SOMETHING YOU'RE GOOD AT

This is one of my rules: if it's well lit, it's not a boutique hotel. A word as overused as boutique needs definitions. Standards. Meaning.

I have been to hotels in the kind of places where the light is some kind of otherworldly painting, where the sun shines so purely that divinity seems obvious, unquestionable. And, somehow, the hotels in these places are dark. In the darkness, one can ignore the corners cut, the cheapness of the design, and get into the vibe. Boutique hotels sell vibe. Feelings. Mood. And the mood is always dark. Boutique hotels are Holiday Inns with better linens and a resident DJ. People will figure this out one day. Except if they listen to me. Except when they read what I have to say about these very hotels in places as diverse as Vietnam. Or Vienna. Or Marrakesh. Or here, in Mexico.

I should be fair. The property here is not a boutique. It is too vast. Over three hundred rooms and suites. Beach-front cabanas. Two storey houses overlooking a manmade lagoon. A full service spa. The boutique part is a kind of hotel within a hotel adjacent to the main building. Dedicated concierge. A hipster cocktail bar serving Asian fusion tapas. And the darkness. It's as if the developers saddled this place with heavier curtains, low wattage light bulbs. If another hurricane strikes this coast, and it will, the boutique part of this resort could easily play the part of morgue. Come stay here in hip surroundings. Death optional.

As it is, "boutique" has gone the way of "brilliant." It doesn't mean anything anymore, if it ever did.

In French, *"concierge"* means janitor. I've always found that funny.

I have been to the Mayan Riviera many times, since before it was branded, and every time the changes and the construction and the development amount to more of the same. A wall of hotels in various shades of white, all promising the same thing, the same "exclusive" thing, all ready for the influx of topless Italians and perky Americans and drunken Brits and newly wealthy Latinos making it rain over the hired help. All discovering a deep-seated desire to rent Sea-Doos and venture a few yards into the ocean. The Sea-Doo thing, at least here, would appear to be lodged into some primordial bit of our DNA. I discovered that here. And in Florida. And in Ibiza. And in Sri Lanka. And Morocco. It's universal. So it must be innate. Conrad would write about Sea Doos were he alive today. Perhaps it's best for him, and for us, that he isn't.

Today, I have to take the spa treatment. I'm obliged. I enjoy saunas but I've grown averse to massages. It took me eight years to realize I don't enjoy being touched by strangers. If I submit, it's for work. And then I pretend to enjoy it. I pretend to enjoy being rubbed with oils or emollients or mud or chocolate or wine. To having this spread over my body while the same New Age pan flute plays in the room while the masseuse goes into her pseudo-religious gobbledygook about "mind" and "self." How did Zamfir become the official soundtrack to massages the world over?

The day is oppressive. The sun's fire reaches down and torches everything. To breathe is to sweat. The manager of the spa greets me at the front door and introduces me to Carlos, the spa concierge. Carlos looks two years removed from an auto body shop, which is unfair of me but it's the image I have of short, young Mexican men with wispy moustaches. He leads me to the locker room and hands me a towel, a bathrobe, and slippers. "This is your locker," he says, opening it up. "I am here for you. I have planned your day with us and, after you change, we will sit in our juice room and discuss your day." He smiles a big smile. "The juice room is right behind us. The one with the leather couches. I will see you there, yes?" And right away I can see the designers of this place, sitting in some corporate park in New Jersey, giggling. Asking any Spanish speaker to say "juice" so many times during the course of their normal workday is not just cruel, it smacks of colonialism.

I thank Carlos. I undress, hoping for, at best, time in a pool with a margarita. Surely that kind of therapy is better for my soul than another massage.

Inside the locker: a brush, creams and lotions, two bottles of mineral water, one sparkling, one still; a shoe shine kit; a shoe horn; a green apple placed perfectly on a slab of what looks to be mahogany. Again, the tyranny of the green apple. Another boutique staple that has lost all meaning. Fruit as décor. As meaning. As cliché.

I wrap the towel around my waist and put the bathrobe on, leaving it untied. I slip my feet into the slippers. And I find Carlos in the juice room. "Please," he says, gesturing to a caramel coloured leather couch. "Please sit."

I do as I'm told. I'm not wearing underwear after all.

He has planned the next four hours of my life. Choice of juices or mineral waters. A soak in a plunge pool. A shower. A Swiss sauna. Another shower. Choice of massage: either Swiss, Thai or Mayan. I go for the Mayan. Go local, I always say. Otherwise, what's the point? Followed by a lunch consisting of soup and tea to heat me up again. And then a quick swim in cold water. And another shower. And then a pedicure / manicure. Topped off with a facial / exfoliation. Lovely. Except for the massage, I could be anywhere in the world. I could be at the urban spa just around the corner from my house.

I accept a mango-papaya juice. It is called "Envigoration." It tastes more of mango than papaya which is just as well. I sign a form. Carlos leads me to a private outdoor plunge pool in a small courtyard. The pool is surrounded by marble walls. The vines from the other side of the walls have just begun their descent. A Roman fountain at the far end. Behind the pool, a large shower with six knobs, four water jets and a rainshower shower head. I can already see that the shower head is too high. A rainshower shower head needs to be at the right height for it to feel like an actual shower head. This one is going to feel wrong.

I walk into the pool and Carlos places my juice on a small tray by the side. He hangs up my bathrobe. "Please," he says. "If you need me, you call my name. The intercom system hears every-thing." He leaves. I look around for proof of this intercom system and I imagine hidden cameras as well. The greater the luxury, the greater the surveillance.

I dunk myself into the pool and wipe my face. I walk over to the side and grab my juice. The water temperature is tepid and feels refreshing in the heat. I'm bored.

I once wrote a story about a spa in the Solomon Islands. Their business went up almost fifty percent after the story was published. I have eaten at great and not so great restaurants in the world's capitals. I have gone whale-watching in Patagonia. I have hunted wild boar in Russia. I went bungee jumping in New Zealand. I once fed a giraffe from my hotel window in Tanzania. I also fed a giraffe in San Diego. I make the world a nicer sounding place than it really is. I sell the world as an endless buffet of eternal extravagance. I visited Bali two months after the terrorist attacks and in the ensuing article managed to mention the carnage just once, in the second paragraph.

I get out of the pool and walk to the shower. I manage to navigate the knobs and water assaults me from all sides. I feel like a student in a protest march in Seoul. Why are those Korean students so angry? They should be happy to live in such a happening place. With good food.

The rainshower shower head produces a good amount of water but it's too high. I step out of the watery assault. Carlos appears. He turns off the water and looks at me, smiling, always smiling. "Sauna?" he asks. "Please, this way."

He holds open the door to the sauna and I enter. The heat of this place sucks the water off my body and then I'm sweating. It's a neat transference of liquid.

The sweat beading on my forehead, the heat inside offers little respite from the day's temperature. A sauna in Mexico doesn't seem so logical. Carlos pushes a button and the room is enveloped in steam.

I take a seat in the corner, I always do in one of these things, and I ease my back against the wall. I wipe my face. A sauna is a sauna is a sauna is a Scandinavian invention is a box of heat is a stupid thing in a country that is nothing but heat. Two days ago, I got smoked out of a little tipi-like structure. A Mayan sauna. I ran out hacking and coughing, the steam burning my lungs. That sauna, at least, wasn't inspired by any Nordic template.

"OK?" Carlos asks.

"Sure," I say. "Gracias."

He leaves the sauna and closes the door and then the steam starts to fly. The hiss of the steam is like the long fuse of a cartoon bomb, something from Saturday morning. Snidely Whiplash chuckles asthmatically as the fuse is lit and our hero faces imminent doom.

I count the tiles on the ceiling. Fourteen across. Sixteen from to back. And then... the hiss of the steam. The tiles on the ceiling. I count them again. And again. And then I realize something awful.

I feel sick. Lost maybe. I develop a headache. I lie down on the bench and dig my thumb into my temple.

I've been here before.

I leave the sauna. I grab my bathrobe and run to the locker. Carlos runs after me, flustered. "Señor?" he calls out. "Sir?"

I ignore him, I barely hear him. He won't stop asking questions. At the locker I reach into my shorts for my cellphone. I dial up the web. I dial up my website and search. And there it is. Six years back. I reviewed this place when it first opened. For *Travel Life.* The same editor. She's given me an assignment to the same place, the same limited focus on one property. No renovations. No improvements. No upgrades. This is the exact same spot offering the same service to the same tribe of people. I'm writing the same story.

I exit the web and call my editor. "Hello?" Esther says. Live from New York....

"Esther, it's Ted."

"Ted," she says, laughing. "Aren't you in Mexico?"

"Esther I've been here," I say.

"Ted, you've been everywhere," she says. "Honestly, where haven't you been?"

"No, listen, I've been here. To this place. To this exact resort. I was in the sauna. The same sauna. For you."

Silence. I can hear her process this. "Are you sure?" she asks.

"Look it up," I say. "Look it up. Same story. Same place. Same angle. Same everything."

Another long silence. "Where are you?"

"Esther, I'm on the fuckin' Mayan Riviera!" I think I'm yelling. "You sent me here when the boom was just starting. To this place. You thought it epitomized the new Mexico. Or something. I'm here for the same reason."

"Isn't that something?" she says. She laughs.

"Why is this funny?"

"Can't you stay somewhere else?"

"And do what?" I ask. All the resorts are the same. There's nothing to add. Not for the story she wants. The place is still booming. End of story.

"You'll think of something," she says.

"Esther don't be unreasonable," I say. "There's nothing here. The new coast is on the Pacific. That's where the interesting stuff is. The story's not here."

"And we did 'Mexico's Wild Coast' just six months ago," she says. Maybe she's understanding what I'm saying.

"I'd like to go home," I say.

"We just wasted a lot of money, then," she says.

Yes. But it's not my money. Or hers really. "So what?" I say. "There's nothing here. Nothing. Nada. I'm going home."

"This is so inconvenient," she says. I hear the tapping of her computer.

"Are you multi-tasking?" I ask.

"I'm not the boss of you," she says.

The next flight to Montreal is in the morning. I make arrangements for transport with the front desk and then call for a cab to take me into town. I head away from the beach and walk to the real town, where the locals live. Mexicans. Migrants who have come from all over the country to work the resorts, to fill the legions of jobs available here. The service economy. We live in a world of those being served and everyone else.

I buy a beef taco from a street cart. At another cart, I buy a stick of mango sprinkled with chili powder. I get a beer. I get a plate of chickin *pibil* and chase that with another beer. The best places in the world are within ten feet of a food cart. That's where the local lives. My taco here, my beer, the kids kicking around a beat-up soccer ball. All more comforting than another three-hundred thread count sheet on a plush mattress. I'm writing the wrong stuff.

In Montreal, the usual hassles of returning home. The mail. The bills. The endless messages on the phone. The empty fridge. The funky smell of an apartment that is both my home and just another bed. The walls of my apartment are bare. A shelf in the hallway that leads to my bedroom labours under the weight of the souvenirs from my travels. I have a thing for snowglobes from unlikely places. I have one from Dubai. I have a well stocked bar. I enjoy *pisco*. And *soju*. And scotch. Alcohol in general.

I fell into travel writing. It wasn't a life's ambition. It happened and for the first few years, jetting around was intoxicating. I had a jet set life, I could work in my pyjamas if need be. In swim trunks. I could go snorkeling and call it work. I won awards. I was proud of my passport. Running out of pages in my passport filled me with immense pride.

And then it wasn't so much. The thought of boarding another aircraft, of checking into another hotel, of waking up in the middle of the night, panicked, unsure of where I was. I was tired of the life. Except that I was good at it. My father had always said, "Find something you're good at and then stick to it." That was all I would need, he said.

He was wrong.

I walk to my neighbourhood bar to meet a friend. We try and catch up once a month, to reclaim our friendship and our pasts and make this city our home again. He has his own company, in software, and he's on the road as much as I am. If not more. Except that he can't stop, no matter how much he wants to, because it's his company he's growing, the travel a direct result of his ambition, his success, and so he keeps going. He complains but it lacks sincerity.

I take a seat at the bar and the bartender pours me a Jack and coke. She does this without asking, she knows me, and I like that. I like that she feels she can assume. She quenches my thirst without a word passing between us.

"Where were you this time?" Lyne asks, placing my drink in front of me.

"Mexico," I say. "Again."

"I've never been," she says.

"I got to this resort and realized I'd already been there," I say.

She laughs. "The horror," she says.

"I left," I say.

She shakes her head. "And you didn't figure this out before?" she asks.

"Not until I got into the sauna," I tell her.

"You lead a crazy life," she says and she walks to the other end of the bar to take another order.

My friend, Bert, walks in and sits next to me and slaps my back. "Good to see you," he says.

"Same," I say.

In the darkness of the bar, I can't tell whether or not Bert is tired. He's almost always tired and his face advertises this with an alarming clarity. I keep trying to get him to try some facial cream, something to relax his face. He has deep-set lines all over, like a topo map of the Grand Canyon. He doesn't care. His appearance is the least of his worries.

"So?" he asks.

Lyne comes over with a vodka tonic. She can quench Bert's thirst as well.

"I'm having doubts," I say.

"This is old news," he says, sipping his drink.

"I need a break," I say.

He puts his arm around my shoulder. "So take one. Do nothing. No one's forcing you to work. Unlike me."

I take my glass and hold it out and Bert's glass touches mine. "I don't know," I say.

"Here's what happened to me," he says. "I was in London. Just a few days ago. And I'm at the hotel bar. I was staying at this small place in Marleybone. All the staff at the bar is Polish. Every single one. I'm at a table with two Frenchmen, an Italian woman, and a guy from Brazil. We're eating these little Indian fusion things. Curried beef in air puffed wonton wrappers. Things like that. Delicious. We're drinking wine. An Australian Shiraz. The bar is full of people. Packed. Loud. God, it was loud. Full. Not a single British accent. I spent four days in London and not one of my meetings was with an actual Brit. I met with two Pakistani guys and that was as close as I got to hearing a Brit talk. Both of them were Oxford boys. The chambermaids in the hotel are all Romanian. The front desk was staffed by Swedes or something."

Why is he telling me this? "So?" I ask.

He takes a sip of his drink. "It just occurred to me that it doesn't matter where you go. You can go anywhere and meet the same people. And when I thought this, I remembered you'd said something very similar like, what, five years ago?"

"Everyone discovers this truth at their own pace," I say.

"I should be doing everything by video conferencing," he says. "That's what I'm thinking."

"But we need the human contact," I say.

"But we need the human contact," he says.

"Even if you hate people," I say.

"What I realized was that everything's cyberspace," he says. "It's all a video game. Or a website. Something."

"This is why I like street food," I say.

"It reminds you," he says.

I nod. "It's the only thing. Otherwise the streets are all the same."

"But that's not true," he says.

"It is," I say.

"Every city I go to is so different. The history's different. The buildings. The culture. No matter what you say. That's where you're wrong. It's just that everyone lives everywhere. The people are the same. Or the kinds of people. But every city is different."

Esther calls in the morning. She wakes me up. "You owe me a story," she says.

"I haven't had my coffee yet," I tell her. I reach over for my alarm clock. It says 7:45. "Esther, why are you working?"

"Who says I'm working?" she says.

"You're calling me about work," I complain. "This is a work-related call."

"I just thought, you know, Ted owes me a story."

"This was not your first thought of the day." I sit up and try to rub the sleep from my eyes. "I'll email you later."

"I have some ideas," she says.

"Fine," I say. "You always do."

"I'll email."

"That's what I said."

She hangs up. Esther is, in many ways, the perfect editor. I can pitch her anything and she'll say yes. I know her magazine as well as she does. I know what not to pitch. And she knows she can send me anywhere and get a good story. We have a relationship. She hates when I have an assignment with another publication. She even admits to jealousy.

I roll over and stare at the clock. It is the same clock I use when I'm on the road. I bought it in Tokyo. Everyone should own one thing bought at an electronics store in Tokyo. I hug my pillow.

After the coffee: I check in with my parents. I call my sister. I spend an hour tidying up the website. I go to the *dépanneur* and buy some juice, a carton of milk, some eggs. I get a loaf of sourdough from the bakery. I pop into the butcher for some steaks, some chicken sausage, a pork tenderloin. I get home, put everything away, and decide to go for a jog. I last half an hour. I pick up a slice of pizza. I stop by the bar for a drink. I go home. I fall asleep on the couch while watching *Simpsons* reruns. Rare is the country where you can not find *Simpsons* reruns on TV. I'm waiting for *The Economist* to create some kind of index based on this.

In almost every hotel room in the world, regardless of size, you can always hear a shower running in the morning. You hear the plumbing. You hear other people, the traffic in the hallway. As I lie here on my couch, I'm realizing how much all of this bothers me.

I once stayed in an eco-lodge in the rainforest of Queensland, Australia. The Rain Tree. In the middle of the night, above the sounds of the birds and insects, I heard someone deposit a very liquid, explosive crap. The thing echoed throughout the forest and the lodge.

Esther emails me asking what I know about Bulgaria. I admit to knowing nothing. Perhaps less than that. She suggests I should start some research.

And reading that, her expectation of this, triggers in me a kind of seismic revulsion. The thought of going anywhere right now is as appealing as watching an innocent man's execution. I decide I'll ignore her email. If something about Bulgaria comes up on TV, I'll switch the channel. If confronted with Bulgarian feta, I'll demand Greek. If someone mentions Bulgaria in conversation, I'll plug my ears and sing. Fuck Bulgaria.

"I think I've lost my passion for the world," I say.

Renata considers this, playing with her straw. Renata is my ex-girlfriend and possibly the only woman I have ever loved. I think I remain friends with her just to torture myself, to remind myself of how attractive a more sedentary life might have been. How sexy.

"Bullshit," she says.

I smile. What other reaction is there to someone who knows you this well? "I'm not joking," I say. "Not really."

"You're bored," she says. She says this to mock me.

"I think so," I reply.

"You really think so?" she asks. The waiter comes by with a large Greek salad and two plates. This is where we always come to eat. We dissect each other's lives over mediocre Greek food served by unhappy, unhealthy-looking waiters.

The waiter leaves. I take a long pull from my beer. "Something's happened to me," I say. "Something happened in Mexico and, I don't know, something happened."

Renata puts her hair behind her ears, takes her fork and attacks her salad. "The world can't possibly be boring," she says. She shoves a forkful of salad into her mouth.

"It is," I say. "That's the thing. It's boring. It's overrated. The world is overrated. There's this monoculture happening and it's erasing all the differences that might make things interesting."

"Bullshit," she says. Again. "That is such crap. The world is not boring. You travel the boring part of the world. You've written about the same people, the same places, the same hotels since I've known you. You're writing for this strata," and here she draws a line way above her head, "that is a monoculture, yes, OK. They travel widely and expect the same stuff in every corner of the globe. It's this tribe, this type, and all the people who want to join in. You've been complaining about these people and these places since we were together. And you keep feeding that machine, you keep writing these stories that could be about anyplace. It's like you have a template. Insert chic resort here. Insert name of cool chef here. Insert quirky but delicious wine list here. Insert interesting or exotic local color here...."

"OK, OK," I say interrupting.

"You just have to explore beyond those manicured grounds, or not go to the same nightclubs, the same restaurants, and you'll see the world is different," she says. "It's why you like street food so much. Look, everyone wears pants but it doesn't mean everyone's the same."

I have no idea what that means. "I'm tired," I say.

"Of what?" she asks, stuffing her mouth with more salad.

"I don't know," I say. The thought of eating now seems like a bad idea.

Renata and I went out for four years. We lived together for two. And during that time, I was establishing myself. And I did. I wrote a book as well, about the globalization of style. I graduated from a dollar a word. I got *Condé Nast.* I wrote for magazines in London, in Australia. I was a talking head on TV. I consulted for hotel chains looking to exploit the boutique niche. When Renata moved in, I basically moved out. It took her two years to understand this. And then she left and my apartment has been haunted by her absence ever since.

"The world is very interesting," she says. "And different. It's just the world you travel in that's boring. You write travel porn. You're good at it."

I would have married her had I realized it was what I wanted to do. "There should be a better word for travel porn," I say.

"The richness of the world is lost on you," she says.

"Stop," I say.

She relaxes. "Sorry," she says.

"I'm not hungry," I say.

"Wait for the waiter," she says. "Then take your souvlaki home,"

I take another pull of my beer.

"I'm sorry," she says again. "It's just that I've seen you like this before."

"No you haven't," I say. She has seen me feign these feelings. But she has never seen me actually suffer because of them. I'm suffering. I admit it. It sounds dramatic, but that's how it feels. How many people like flying at sunset on north-south routes? And then angle to get a seat on the right side of the plane so they can watch the horizon go from purple to aqua to yellow to peach to pink? I do. This is something I do. I appreciate beauty. I love the way Renata's nose is just a touch too large for her face. How her hair falls over her forehead, barely touching her eyelashes. I love the blue of the Mediterranean. The riot of colors on the native ponchos in Bolivia. The difference between *chapattis* in Tanzania and India.

"What do you want to do?" she asks.

"Give me a hint," I say.

Esther talks me into Bulgaria. Somehow. She says the Brits have discovered the coast of the Black Sea. Meaning it's already ruined. She offers me double my rate just to get me there and write it up quickly. She's sending an Italian photographer to meet me in Sofia. Esther wants Sofia and the coast. Her art director arranged for a model at one of the hotels. Maybe this is a cover. Esther wants to announce

Bulgaria as next-big-thing before anyone else. I tell her I'm doing this for the money and because I owe her. She mocks me.

Lufthansa from Montreal to Frankfurt and then a quick change to Sofia. At the gate in Montreal, I watch my fellow passengers board. I watch. I stand watching. The final boarding call comes over the PA. I watch the gate attendant make the call. I watch her. I watch her search the gate area. She announces my name. She consults with her colleagues. My names comes over the PA once again. I watch the gate attendant look at her watch. She shrugs. And I don't move.

THE KING OF WIMPS

When my wife started shouting at me every time I returned home late from work I knew I'd become my father. This is for real. Never mind that my father and I both have two kids. Or that we are both surprised–and maybe even mildly disappointed–with the people we became. This is superficial crap. But there was something about the way my wife yelled it at me for coming home late that just floored me. I took my punishment, went into the bathroom and stared at myself in the mirror and admitted, finally, that yes, I had become my father.

My children are fine. I don't have a problem there. I love them. It's a love that makes you ache. In a good way. Without them, I'm not me. I'm nothing. It doesn't bother me that I don't think this way about my wife. Who I love as well but just not in the same way. Obviously.

The children are nine and six. The older one, Mason, has a bit of a ruffian thing to him and for the first year or so he really disliked his younger brother. He made things difficult. But now he is as protective of his sibling as he is of his toys. Meaning he must really have his back.

The younger one, Kris, is all about impressing his brother. He will do whatever Mason asks him to, even if he knows he can't. He is fearless in a way that is both admirable and scary, frankly, especially if you're me. I'm not fearless at all. I'm the king of wimps. If you don't believe me, consider this: I want to be more like him. A six-year old.

I take them to this park. It's two blocks from our house and last year the city outfitted it with new playground equipment. There are no swings, which seems wrong and anal to me but that must be what the specialists are recommending these days. The playgound equipment is completely different from when I was a kid. The only thing that seems to have survived the playground specialists and the bureaucrats' fear of lawsuits is the slide. I prefer the modern slides. The plastic doesn't get as hot in the sun. How often did we burn the skin on the backs of our legs from a sun-baked slide when we were kids? Never, probably, but I carry this memory with me and it's a vivid one.

Normally, I let the kids have the run of the park and I sit on a bench that gets good shade and I read the paper. And after every story, I look up and see that everything is right with the world and go back to reading about the parts of the world where it isn't. I forgot the paper today.

The kids run toward the giant jungle gym-like contraption, screaming with joy. The thing is a giant pyramid with a spider's web of chains that lead to the top. It's at least twenty-feet high. How this is safer than a set of swings escapes me.

I take my regular seat and wonder where the paper was in the house. The paper is not something that I normally forget. I don't like the news but I like to know what's going on. Ignorance may be bliss but it's not fun. Mason practically runs up the jungle gym and I stay in my seat despite my instinct for seeing disaster everywhere. Kris follows him. A woman takes a seat on the bench next to me. "Are they yours?" she asks. She is young, perhaps in her late twenties, and her auburn hair falls over her shoulders in a messy surrender. Her green eyes are lost to the bags under them. I'm thinking she's a single mom. Which makes her both sexy and sexless to me, some-thing I can't explain but that I could talk about with a group of guys and a few beers over the better part of an evening.

"Yup," I say. "Where's yours?"

She looks around and points to a boy by the water fountain. "He's six," she says.

"He looks very big for six," I say, not because it's true, but it's a way for me to say something neutral, non-judgemental. I've been screwed by saying the wrong thing to a parent before. Like, he looks short for his age. Or, is she alright? Or, what a lovely girl. Better to stay safe.

"He's pretty average," she says.

Then I would get along well with him, I think. "No one's average," I say. "Everyone's special."

Mason lets out a boastful yelp. He's at the top of the pyramid. Kris is one level below complaining about it since he knows Mason will not let him anywhere near the top. He's very King of the Castle that way.

"That's quite a line," the woman says. "That's like Miss America special."

And with this I do a half turn. "You can never be too careful when you're talking about other people's kids," I say. "You just don't know where the sensitivities lie." How wrong is it to think impure thoughts of another mother while you're looking out for your kids? Even if the mother is single? Is it a guy thing or am I a suck? Why must that question always lead to the same answer?

She reaches into her purse and takes out a cigarette. "Mind if I smoke?"

"You can smoke here," I say. "God knows you can't smoke anywhere else."

She offers one to me. "You want one?" she asks.

I beg off. I quit long enough ago to not miss it but not long enough ago to know how much I'd enjoy it. "Thanks, no. I'll live through yours vicariously."

She lights her cigarette and we watch the kids. Her son runs up the slide and rappels down a pole. Mason notices this and I can tell he's trying to figure out what's more fun: staying atop the pyramid or joining the other boy. He makes his way for the other boy. Kris takes his brother's place atop the pyramid but even at six he can sense this victory is hollow.

"That thing freaks me out sometimes," I say. "They've never gotten hurt but sometimes I watch them up there and I imagine the worst things. I imagine my son falling off the top and getting tangled in the chains and breaking his arm. Or his head. Something."

"They're pretty safe, I think," she says.

"One time, I imagined this accident so vividly, I stayed under the pyramid the whole time. My son got caught in the chains and his arm came off. It came right off and squirted this cartoon blood and I was left holding the arm and he was running around with this geyser shooting out of a hole just above his elbow." And I think right away perhaps I shouldn't admit something like this to a stranger, even one that has offered me a cigarette.

"We all worry," she says, exhaling. "It's built in."

"I'm the same way around dogs," I say. "I can't help but think they're going to tear one of my kids limb from limb. I have a vivid picture of my kid's head in the jaws of a pit bull. I don't know where it comes from."

I fully expect the woman to get up and leave. I would. "I don't have that kind of luxury," she says. Oddly.

I want one of her cigarettes but this would set me back so far I can't even fathom the distance. Far. You're never an ex-smoker once you quit, just a smoker who doesn't smoke. But smoking in front of the kids sounds cool.

"Sorry," I say. "My imagination just gets the better of me."

Mason plays with her son. They run up the slides and slide down while the other is running up and laughing. Kris stays atop the pyramid watching them, knowing that he's missing out on the most fun in the history of the world. He'll join them shortly.

And will be the first to cry. Three kids together means alliances, recriminations. And that the crying isn't far behind.

"You live nearby?" she asks. "The boys seem to be getting along. I'm always looking for friends."

I'm a manager. A bureaucrat. This is what I do. I manage things. In insurance. I work in insurance ensuring that our sales are on target. I don't set targets I only ensure that the people below me reach them. My title is Senior Manager, Financial Quality. Fucked if I know what that means, but being a manager comes with small privileges and when you work in a giant office, privilege is everything. My benefits are better. I'm treated slightly better by the executive class. Sometimes I get to travel. I get a gym membership. And then there's being responsible. This is the bad part about being a manager. I am responsible for a department. I have people who come to me to update me on the work being done. I have to attend a lot of meetings.

The modern office meeting is tedious and silly and so far removed from anything I imagined myself doing when I was a kid that the whole thing seems like a joke to me. This is a thought I have at least once a day: I can't believe this is my life.

Growing up, I wanted to be a lawyer. Excessive television watching made it seem glamorous. And then the reality of the amount of work appeared to me like a vision of the apocalypse and I wandered through college with no real goal but to get a degree. I dabbled in everything. And so I ended up in insurance.

What is the line from our swinging in trees to going to wars to discovering continents to the fucking office meeting? Is the line a direct one?

And then, once a year, the performance review. A more useless activity I cannot imagine. As a senior manager, I have to review the junior managers. And as a senior manager, the depth of my own review is, well, deeper. I have a pre-review from HR. And once I've done that, my direct supervisor is given a report on which to base her review of me. And then we're supposed to meet. But not before HR has their way with me. The HR people love performance reviews. It is the only time they feel important.

And of all the questions I have to ask and be asked this is the question I hate the most: where do you see yourself in five years? I mean, do you trust anyone with this kind of plan? Five years? Ask me about five minutes, maybe. Five hours is possible. But five years? Are you kidding? In five years? Let's see. I want more pay for less work. How's that sound? I want an easier life, I want a bigger house, and I want to get to the green in two maybe. On a 475 yard dogleg left par five. How does that sound? I want the kind of job where I can ask this inane fuckin' question to people who don't have a clue what *they* want to do in five years. I don't trust anyone who knows how to answer this. I don't ask it when I'm doing my reviews. Ever.

So, here I am, sitting at my pre-review and I get the question. And this is my answer: "In five years, my kids will be five years older. I'll probably have more of a paunch. I hope my wife and I are still together. I'm hoping maybe there'll be a new car in the picture. I'd like to redo the backyard patio. I also want to score a hat trick in my beer league and maybe in five years I'll be able to manage that. Oh, and I'd like to go to Japan."

She sits there, blankly staring. Surely, I deserve a smile or something. "No really," she says. She pushes a lock of her blond hair off her forehead.

"I'm telling you."

"This is serious," she says. "You need to tell me. I have to write something down."

"Japan. Did you get that part?"

She leans toward me, almost as if she's going to put her hand on my leg. Now, that would be cool. "A lot rides on these things," she says. I doubt this is the right time to tell her I have a thing for Irish women. Her last name's O'Connor. So, I'm pretty sure she's Irish. She has that icy blue eyes, auburn hair, freckled face look and it makes me weak. "I have to write reports and they go to the group VP. And your direct supervisor. They take my report and, to be honest, that's it. They don't really do any other kind of prep. My report is your final review for all intents. Help me out."

"Is my job on the line?"

She leans back again. "That's not what I'm saying."

I take a deep breath. "I want to grow with this company. This company's growing and I want to grow with it. In five years I want to lead my division. I'm aiming for the executive suite."

She scribbles furiously into her notebook. She ticks off three boxes on the chart. I'm sure she has just noted that I'm ambitious. For fuck's sake.

"I want to lead this company to higher levels of greatness," I say.

She smiles. She has perfect, perfectly whitened, teeth. "OK," she says. "Whoa there."

This time, I make it a point not to take the newspaper to the park. I take my seat at the bench and watch my kids take their place upon the jungle gym. Their normal places. "Hi," she says. It's her. I can tell without even turning my head. I turn my head. She has a cigarette in her mouth. Her hair is up in a ponytail. She'd look younger if it weren't for the lines on her face. What has she been through to look so ragged? Because underneath the lines, she's amazingly beautiful. It's as obvious as a sunrise.

"How's the kid?" I ask.

He's running to the pyramid and when he gets there he scrambles up and shoots right past Kris. He joins Mason at the top and they push themselves around. "Be careful!" I yell.

"He's got a built-in safety valve," she says. "He's always on the edge but he never gets hurt."

"That thing's just so high," I say.

"They'll be fine," she says. "I'm Jen." She extends her hand and I shake it. Her hands are rough. Like she's a carpenter or something.

"I'm Vik," I say.

"I'm guessing that's short for something really long," she says.

I nod. "It's just easier. That's what everyone calls me." Her son starts pulling at Mason's shirt, trying to get him off the pinnacle. "Crap!"

"Stan, honey!" she yells. "No pulling, OK?"

Stan stops. A boy that listens to his mother. Now I'm convinced Jen is a single mom. "I just see the fall," I say. "I can't help it. I see the fall and the broken bones and the head. I have a thing for head injuries. That's the big worry."

"Mom!" Stan calls. "I want to be on top!"

"Should I get him down?" I ask.

"No, no," she says, putting out her cigarette in the sand. "They'll work it out. Stan! You wait your turn." Jen turns to me. "Did you have an accident as a child?" she asks.

I had a very safe childhood. My father was overprotective. This is what I want to avoid. "No. Not one. I've never broken a bone in my body. I think that's why I worry about broken bones so much. I don't know what it feels like."

"Imagine all the bones that break in the world every day," she says. "Imagine how many bones are breaking right now."

And I do. I can imagine it. When I was younger, a horny teenager, I'd often ask my friends to imagine the amount of people having sex… right now. And now. And now. "And dying," I say.

"You really are morbid, Vik," she says.

"And being born," I say.

"And having sex," she says. "Can you imagine that?"

The result of my performance review: a promotion. I get a bigger office. More pay. More of everything, really. And for what? For being ambitious? For faking ambition.

The new office is next to my old one. An upgrade in the furniture and the square footage. The wood on the desk is darker, mahogany perhaps. It's bigger too so I can make more of a mess. I'm messy. A title change. Director, Financial Quality. I've gained a division or something. My boss comes in and congratulates me. "You deserve it," she says. How often has she said this? "Your work is stellar. We're all impressed with what you've been doing. We look forward to working with you in this new role. We know you'll do a fantastic job." Who is we? What cabal is she referring to?

"Thank you," I say. "This feels good."

"Settle in," she says. "In a weird way, the job gets easier almost. More pressure. But less work. Funny, eh?" She laughs and I laugh along. I feel ridiculous.

She makes to leave my new office and at the door, she turns around. She surveys the office. "Our growth the past two years have been quite incredible. You're a big reason for it."

I have nothing to add to this. I shrug.

"I'll be by later today," she says. "We can talk about our goals."

The chair is more comfortable. It's cushier. It swivels in more ways and more directions than my old chair. A new computer. For what? Why should I have a new computer? Why does every day at this job make me feel like more of a fraud?

I call my wife at her office and tell her about the promotion. "That's lovely," she says.

"We should celebrate," I say.

"Let's wait for the weekend," she says. "And then maybe we'll have a picnic with the kids. And we'll get a sitter and go out Saturday night. On me."

We pack a lunch and head to the park. I've been at my new job for two days and nothing has changed. At least I don't think it has. Except that I'm getting new business cards. And I have yet to read the new manual for my new computer or study the new passwords that give me more access to more company secrets.

The kids run toward the pyramid. My wife chooses a spot on a shady part of the grass and lays out a blanket. I put the picnic basket on top. At the bench, I see Jen, smoking, watching Stan. For whatever reason I want a cigarette now more than ever. I scratch my throat. I remember that my father stopped smoking when I hit ten.

Jen is wearing a yellow t-shirt and jean shorts. Her legs are fatter than I realized. She doesn't look my way.

My wife takes out a bottle of white wine, a California Cab, from the basket. Two plastic wine cups. She lays out the food on the blanket and arranges plates. She calls out to the kids. Fried chicken. Cole slaw. Corn on the cob. She uncorks the wine. I love my wife's fried chicken. She calls the kids again. She serves the food on the plates. I take another peek at Jen and she's watching Stan as he watches my kids run toward us. As he listens to the laughter of my boys.

TWO STAR

1

She is an actress. It says so on her business card. Her occupation
is not so much a job as a fact. It informs all of her decisions, her
actions, the words that spill from her mouth. She dresses as she
thinks an actress should. Her walk, whether shopping for eggs, or
entering a director's office, is that of an actress. Or her interpreta-
tion of how an actress should walk. She's acting like an actress.
This will lead to bigger movies. To fame. To stalking. She wants to
be stalked. She wants to find out things about herself on websites.
She wants to exit a car at a happening Korean BBQ joint and be
assaulted by flashbulbs.

She sits alone, at a table near the middle of the room. Her waiter
has delivered a club soda with lime. She awaits her green salad, no
dressing, oil and vinegar on the side. Her large, round sunglasses
hide the top half of her face. Her dark hair falls gently over her
shoulders. She wears a bright pink and red floral print dress. The
orange clutch rests on the table, next to the cutlery. Her cellphone
sits beside it.

The room is in that half-and-half light that signals mediocrity
in a restaurant. The fake chandeliers could use dusting. The carpet
is a rust-colored, threadbare pile. There's a funk to the place, a
smell that hints at decades of spilled drinks, excessive frying and
bad perfume. There are businesspeople in this room but no signs
of wealth. Or power. This is middle management territory. The
martinis here are as wet as a baby's mouth.

She knows this and yet she comes here still. She doesn't deserve
the fancy places yet, the rooms where people don't so much eat

but crane their necks to see who's sitting at the next table. This is not the kind of place that sees table-hopping. She comes here to remind herself of her station but also to pick herself up. She comes here to feel superior.

Jones enters with two colleagues and a client from the East Coast. He runs his hand through his hair, takes in the room and sighs a disappointed sigh. The client requested they eat here, speaking of the memories this place held for him. The client was important. Jones begged him to reconsider. "Simon's is the place," he had said. "Everyone's talking about it. I can get us in." But the client insisted. And the client is always right. Even when he's not.

Jones and his party were taken to a booth in the corner of the room. They were going to talk numbers, try and nail down a deal that had loitered for months. Jones was going to close this. He wanted to get it done before the appetizers. And if this didn't work, he was going to get drunk and tell the client he was an asshole.

They sit at the booth. Jones studies the room, shaking his head. I can't believe this place, he thinks. It doesn't feel right. This isn't me. The waiter places a menu before each of them and places the wine list in the middle of the table. Jones notices a yellow stain on the tablecloth and wonders whether he should slide the wine list over to cover to it. He doesn't.

"I don't need to look at this," the client laughs.

"What if it's changed?" one of Jones' colleagues asks.

"This place doesn't change," the client says. "That's why I like it."

Jones thinks, if our evolution had depended on this guy, we'd still be living in caves. He can hear the chatter of the middle management types in the room speaking their conspiratorial talk. Boomers in ill-fitting suits, the younger types eyeing the Boomers with a combination of pity and loathing. Like hyenas watching lions kill a wildebeest. The greyhairs, their sorrow etched into the lines on their faces. Especially when they laugh, their mortality reflected in every bite, every chew, every swallow. These are the walking dead, Jones thinks. These are the people the system screwed. All of them. Ambitions thwarted by the lack of ambition. He shudders.

He notices her. She sits amidst the weeds like a garden lily. "The only thing I'll warn you about are the martinis," the client says. "Damned place can't make a decent martini."

"Well, I'm leaving," the other colleague jokes.

"Check please," the client laughs.

Jones recognizes her but can't place the face. He dives deep into his memory. High school. College. Grad school. Work. Travels. Neighbourhood. Wife's friends. Nina. Linda. Corey. Elaine. Frannie. Yaz. Jane.

Another waiter arrives, his red vest barely containing the years of alcohol abuse. "Gin and tonic," the client says. "All around. And stiff. Tell Ricky to make 'em stiff."

"And should I tell Ricky who's ordering?" the waiter asks.

"He'll know," the client says. "Who else orders a stiff gin and tonic?"

Jones is not a gin man but he doesn't care. He wants to get the deal done. The sooner the better. He wants to be the hero. He'd eat glass if he knew it would close the deal.

He's seen her on television. She's been in some commercials. The kind of ad he'd always thought he was ignoring. She's been an extra on some TV show. He's beginning to place the face. He's staring.

She catches his stare and smiles. He's cute, she thinks. He's slumming it here. He's too well-dressed. He's a successful man, she thinks. Meaning whatever he's discussing is too important for the office or for a high-end restaurant. They don't want to be seen. This is a deal they need to close in anonymity.

She can tell that he recognizes her but can't quite place her. She gets that a lot. It's her reminder that she has yet to achieve anything memorable. Her ambition is nothing less than to etch herself into the public's memory. To be famous enough to do Japanese commercials. She wants the kind of immortality only a certain level of fame can bring. She doesn't need to be a legend. But she needs to be a star.

She understands the dynamics of his table already. He's the alpha. But the older man sitting across from him holds the hammer. He's the one with the money. The other two are nothing but entourage. Scribes to the transaction. Her salad arrives. "Thank you," she says to the waiter.

"Will there by anything else?" he asks.

"I will let you know," she says looking up to him, smiling. She has that beaming, million-watt smile down. She's good at what she does. "Thanks."

The salad will go uneaten. She already knows this. She's not hungry. She rarely is these days. Her impending food issue is as inevitable as an ocean's tide. She knows the worries and the troubles that fame brings. She pours the oil and vinegar into a small bowl and mixes them and then dresses her salad. She puts her fork down. He's married, but cute. And he keeps looking at me.

Their drinks arrive. The client holds his glass up and the rest follow. "Let's get this puppy done," he says.

"Amen to that," one of the colleagues says and the glasses come together.

Jones drinks and the sting of the gin catches him by surprise. "Christ," Jones says, putting his glass down. He hates gin. He can't stand that he's in this place, this one, drinking gin of all things. Did all of this make him a whore? Not that it mattered.

The client laughs. "See? They know me," he says.

Jones sneaks another peak at the actress to see if she has seen his mishap and it's obvious she has. She smiles at him and he shrugs and smiles back. It was some kind of tampon thing, he thinks. The commercial.

"I mean it, Jones," the client says.

Jones looks at him. "You mean what?" he asks, a bit startled.

"Let's do it."

Jones composes himself. He cradles his drink. "I told the boys here I wanted it done before we order," he says. "Before they bring the rolls."

"He did," one of the colleagues says.

"What's been the hold up?" the client asks.

"Legal had some issues," Jones lies. "I've worked that out with them. I don't want this thing held up by periods and commas."

"Damn lawyers," the client says.

"I have the papers in here," he says, tapping his chest. "In my pocket. We haven't changed a thing. I didn't need to bring a brief-case. It's all here. The numbers work for us. We're excited to move forward. To start implementation. We fully believe this is going to be mutually beneficial. It's going to startle people. PR is ready to go with this. We've all worked hard to get to this place and make this work."

"And this took six months?" the client asks. He downs his drink.

"I know," Jones says. "I'm just as frustrated as you are. Let's just consider everything up to now foreplay."

The waiter reappears and the client orders another drink.

"Well, shit," the client says. "I usually get right into it. Bugs the hell out of the wife."

Jones could tell him right now the real problem, the unreasonable demands that have emanated from the client's office. He could. But then he remembers the potential windfall this deal will bring him. He thinks about that nice piece of land two hours north of the city, waiting for the down payment. The prize. "It doesn't matter," Jones says. "We're here now. We're prepared to consummate this thing and run with it."

"We need this too," the client says.

"I have a pen," Jones says.

The waiter arrives with the client's drink. Jones takes a quick peek at the actress. She holds her glass up to him. She's great looking, he thinks.

2

She knows the role means risking everything. The part calls for nudity and sex and the kind of psychological turmoil that can scar someone for years. Her agent says this is her big break. A mid-budget thriller. Some minor A-List actors. Lots of screen time. She's the second female lead. This is a step up the ladder. This is a different rung. "You're perfect for this one," the agent says over the phone. "I worked my ass off to get you the audition. Because I know you can nail this one. I know it."

She sips her coffee. "It's me," she says.

"That's what I'm saying," the agent says.

"I can feel her inside me," she says.

"It's not an open call," the agent says. "It's just five of you. Five girls reading for the part. But it's you. Two of the other girls I know. They don't stand a chance."

"And the other two?" she asks. She finds a bench and sits down.

"I don't know them," he says. "They must be new."

"Find out about them," she says.

"I'm working it," he says.

"Everything you can."

"I'm on it. I'm telling you this."

"OK," she says. She will audition. She understands the system. "The script sucks," she says.

"It's not, baby," he says. "This thing has real potential."

"Fuck off," she says. "It's formulaic."

"Everything is formulaic," he says. "Every fucking script follows a formula. That's how things get made."

"I'm naked half the time," she says. She says this loud enough that passers-by turn their heads.

"Two scenes," he says. "Maybe three."

"They're long scenes," she says.

He sighs. "Is this going to be an issue?" he asks.

She thinks. She has to do this. The director is good. Maybe he can bring the script up. It's not some straight-to-video crap. Could do half-decent box office. The screen time. She's impressed by the screen time. "I don't care," she says. "No, it won't be an issue."

3

Twenty-four acres in the mountains. A brook. A large meadow, once grazing land for horses, now covered with tall grass and wild flowers. His wife can already picture an English garden, a stone path leading up from the meadow to the house. He wants some flat-topped Frank Lloyd Wright-type ranch house and she's amenable. Her brother-in-law is an architect with an affinity for stone walls and wraparound floor-to-ceiling windows.

"I want a green house," she says, as they picnic by the brook. He refills her wine glass.

"Green-ish," he says.

"Chuck says we can go full green," she says. "Chuck's been designing this LEED-certified stuff in the city."

"It adds up," he says. "Green's the colour of money."

"But it's not that much more," she says. "I want to do this right."

He agrees with her. "Fine, fine," he says. He doesn't want this dream deferred by his wife's causes. Theory is so much easier than reality. "I just want the house I've always seen in my head," he says.

"You will, honey," she says. "Chuck listens. He's very sympathetic. He's not your typical architect."

He tears a piece off the loaf of bread and spreads some pâté. "This is going to be our dream house," he says.

She squeezes his leg. "I want the kind of place we can pass down," she says. "I want our kids to pass it along to their kids."

"So we'll need kids first," he says.

"We'll need kids first," she says.

"We're building a foundation," he says, chewing his bread.

"Exactly," she says. She sips her wine.

"Let's see what Chuck says. We'll go as green as possible. Let's not spoil this land."

"Chuck's into harmony. He's almost Buddhist when it comes to this stuff."

He stands up, stares off toward the meadow. He feels the contentment of a man who cannot see the limits of his own land. He understands how primal the feeling is. This is the feeling of kings. Of emperors. "I love this place," he says.

She looks up at him. "You worked hard for it."

He smiles. He was persistent. If persistence equals hard work, then yes, he worked hard. He can imagine a small pond, a swimming hole, stocked with fish. He can imagine spending hours by the water, drinking beer. He can imagine the view from the bedroom, down toward the city. "We should camp here," he says. "Really get a feel for the place."

"I hate camping," she says.

"Me too." He walks onto a rock in the brook. The water rushes past him, sounding like chimes playing in the wind. "I never liked camping. But I want to spend the night here."

"When?" she asks.

"Tonight," he says. "We'll drive into town. Buy a stove and a tent. We'll roast hot dogs or something. I want to experience this land. Our land."

"I have nothing to wear," she says.

"We'll buy something. Sweatpants," he says. "I want to make love to you in a tent on our land."

He looks at her and sees her hesitation.

"In the morning, we'll drink bad coffee and walk around. Discover the place."

And then she smiles and he returns it. "I haven't fucked in a tent since high school," she says.

"Yes, but we're going to make love," he says.

They clean up and pack the trunk and head into town. They find a cheap tent and some chunky sleeping bags in a small hardware store. They purchase a gas stove, a flashlight, some matches, candles. They buy inflatable pillows. They walk across the street to a grocery store and buy hot dogs and buns and some mustard. He throws a can of beans into the cart and finds a can-opener near the beer. They buy another bottle of wine. They find some instant coffee and powdered milk.

Around the corner, they walk into a clothing store and buy sweatpants and t-shirts and sweatshirts. He buys a pack of wool socks. He squeezes his wife's ass as the cashier rings up the bill.

They return to the property and set up camp in a corner of the meadow. He watches his wife lay the ground sheet and falls in love with her again. They set up the tent and he goes into the woods in search of kindling for the fire. This is all mine, he thinks. After an hour, he has found enough wood for a week's stay. He clears a bit of the ground and kicks at the dirt. He surrounds the clearing with small stones. "I am fire man!" he announces.

The sun sets and the sky shimmers with stars. They sit by the fire, drinking wine, burping up the hot dogs. They stare into the sky and see their future. He nuzzles her neck and her hands move over his chest and then they are lying on the ground and never quite make it into the tent until much later. Until he feels the pinprick of a mosquito on his naked ass.

4

She has returned to the restaurant when she can. She got the part in the thriller but her role was cut back in rewrites. Less nudity but less screen time too. Her character, shorn of the complexity she found alluring in the previous draft, gets killed off at the beginning of the second act. It was for the best, she's convinced herself. Everyone else in that movie was an asshole, a has-been and a never-will-be.

The movie's release date has been pushed back. Her agent found her another commercial, for dishwashing liquid, and says he has a lead on another one, for a travel website. This is where I am right now, she thinks. This is the life of an actress.

She wears her hair up, a large yellow bandana covering her forehead. She wears a white button-down shirt and khakis. She sips a club soda. Searching the room.

She sees her cellphone vibrate on the table and answers it. "I've got you an audition," her agent says.

"What kind?" she asks.

"It's big," he says. "Huge budget. Hundred mil."

Her ears get hot. "And?"

"It's a good role," he says. "No one's really attached yet."

"Meaning it's a fishing expedition," she says.

Her agent mentions a director's name. Her ears burn. She sips her drink. Her salad arrives. "Hello?" he says.

"He's doing it?" she asks.

"Signed, sealed," the agent says.

The man from last month walks by her. He is led to a table by one of the windows. She sees him alone. "What's the role?"

"The wife. Tormented. Supportive. It's kind of typical stuff."

He's still alone.

"Lots of special effects," the agent continues. "Car chases. It's a buddy movie. So they don't want a big name for the wife."

"So they want me," she sighs.

"So they want someone like you. Look, this could be huge."

"That's what you always say."

"Come to my office," he says. "I want to show you some outfits you should wear to the audition."

"I can dress myself," she says.

"This has to be perfect," he says.

She always hates to admit that he's right. When the dynamic of their relationship is so obvious. She hates her lack of power. More than anything else, she wants power.

"When?"

"When what?"

"When's the audition?"

A waiter brings the man a scotch. From her vantage, it looks like scotch. Maybe bourbon.

"Next week," the agent says. "Just come by. Say two?"

She checks her watch. She has an hour. She hangs up. She mixes the oil and vinegar and pours it on her salad. She takes a deep breath and stands. She walks over to the man.

"Hi," she says. He looks up, startled. Lost.

"Please, have a seat," he says.

"You were here a month ago," she says. She sits and holds out her hand. "I'm Judy."

"Sam," he says. "You're an actress, aren't you?" he asks.

"Yes," she says. "I'm surprised you noticed."

"I tried to place your face," he says. "I saw you and I recognized your face and then I remembered a commercial."

She smiles. "Oh? Which one?"

"I think it was for tampons," he says, lowering his voice. She finds his embarrassment endearing.

"One must pay the bills," she says.

"I didn't mean anything by it," he stammers.

"Did your deal work out?" she asks, saving himself from whatever it is that renders men idiots at the mention of feminine hygiene.

"What deal?" he asks.

"The deal. The last time," she says. "I had the whole scene pegged. You. Your underlings. Your client. This restaurant. The anonymity of the deal in a crappy restaurant. Very smart."

"It was the client's idea," he says. "Yes. We closed it. It's working out."

His watch is large and chunky and expensive. "And what brings you back?" she asks. She knows the answer. Or wants to know. She anticipates it and as he considers the question her excitement grows.

"I don't know," he lies.

"Because this isn't your kind of place," she says.

"And what kind of place would that be?" he asks.

"You're too successful to come here," she says. "Look around. This place is beneath your station."

"What is my station?" he asks.

"Don't be an asshole."

The waiter brings her salad and another club soda. He places them in front of her. Sam asks for another scotch.

He sighs. "It's quiet," he says.

"It sucks," she says. "I come here because it's all I deserve right now."

She wants him to admit something. She wants him to say it. She knows he's married and this doesn't bother her. "I was here last week, too," he says. He wasn't. He hasn't been here since the meeting. But he wants to play.

"I was filming," she says. "I was stripped to my panties for two weeks, painted with grime. Screaming. Crawling on all fours."

"Glamorous," he says.

"It's what I do," she says.

The waiter returns with his drink. Sam cradles the glass. "I was here the week before that, too," he says.

"On all fours," she says, smiling.

Sam takes a sip of his drink. "I'm married," he says. And this might be interesting, he thinks. Or maybe not.

She points to his finger. "You're wearing it."

"And I love my wife," he says. "We just bought a place in the mountains. We have plans." And then he asks himself the question. What's more important: the house in the mountains? Or this mixed up B-List actress throwing herself at him?

"So why did you come here?" she asks. She stares at him. She takes off her sunglasses to reveal ice blue eyes. She senses his discomfort. She can feel the mileage that has brought him here. She feels her heart beating through her shirt. And she feels a sense of power over him. I can do this, she thinks. I'm going to get this part and do this movie and I'm going to be a star. And then I'll never have to come to this restaurant ever again.

THE WHITE PANTS

A warm spring day, a slight breeze, kites floating in the sky. Children played soccer in the field. Young couples holding hands and talking about their happiness. Kids on swings, pushed by adoring fathers. This was the scene of the disaster.

White pants and a loose bowel.

The accident occurred without effort. The shock of being so naked before so many. He had felt like a naked man in a glass box. And something less than a man.

He's convinced that his girlfriend at the time never recovered from the sight and left him because of it. How can one get over such a scene? The horror of an unpleasant affiliation. And he doubts if he has recovered fully from it. If the bad luck that followed the episode was somehow connected to it. If the event was a kind of unpleasant emanation that produced everything that followed.

There are no tangibles in life, he thinks. Life is illusory. It is full of bad luck and inconveniences. Like an erection that won't go away, a beautiful woman says, "I'm yours." Like the dog that loves you until one day it decides to bite your face. Like Britney. Nothing.

He is not an existentialist though once in college, he performed in a play by Sartre. He was not a pessimist before the incident. He was happy. He enjoyed life. He had a good job, one that fulfilled him. He had a woman he could imagine much joy with.

He had one pair of white pants. Jeans might have saved him. His beloved brown cords surely. But it was warm, it was spring, and the sun rose in the sky like a sorcerer conjuring tube tops and hot pants.

The day was an eruption, the start of a line of fate that would see him lose everything. His employer went bankrupt. His father died. His sister got spiritual, discovered Buddhism, moved to Nova Scotia and was paralyzed from the neck down in a surfing accident. His brother became a criminal defense attorney. His best friend married a woman who stabbed him in the foot before being diagnosed as bipolar. His dog made love to his suede couch. He developed an allergy to chocolate. His car was pulverized by a sizeable portion of a giant elm during a wind storm. His apartment building had to be abandoned after a sinkhole was discovered in the parking garage.

He has thought much about fate and the unexpected directions life can take. What are these things that make up my life, he thinks. I gave my dog away. I don't have a good job. The pride of my life is my plasma screen TV. I can watch late night talk shows in high definition. I have two pairs of shoes. I wheeze. I get too much excitement at the thought of "all you can eat buffets."

He wants to see the episode as a sign, not a confirmation. He wants to shake a fist at the karma that sits in this park. He wants to own that day because he knows the day owns him. He wants to be able to say he doesn't feel sorrow. Or pity. Or a deep and abiding hurt. He wants to wake up to a soundtrack of happy music. No oboes. He wants to love the world. He wants the world to love him.

He finds it ironic and painful that white pants are so in right now. As if the world is mocking him. As if the world really cares what happened at this spot two years ago. He would like to think he has an effect on the world. He doesn't believe in fate. Or, he doesn't want to.

By the soccer field, some ten feet from his accident, a young couple lie in the grass, groping. It's a very *From Here to Eternity* moment and he watches as they roll through the grass like lovers from a slow mo fantasy sequence in a comic television movie. They roll onto the spot. He knows it's the spot because he can feel them crush his spirit.

There are children in this park. He doesn't feel the young couple's affections are appropriate here. And then he imagines that he is the one rolling around, with someone, anyone, and the thought of it arouses in him a hopeless optimism. And then he sits on a bench ashamed, clutching at his stomach. I'm being so dramatic, he thinks. I'm the star of a movie and the movie's called *Losertron*.

A soccer ball approaches the lovers and a kid comes over to retrieve it. He's no older than ten. He's decked out in the billboard-as-uniform of some European soccer power. He's even wearing cleats. He picks up the ball and watches the couple. He studies them. He cocks his head sideways like a bird mesmerized by seed. And then he throws the soccer ball at them. He doesn't even throw it hard. It's as if he's conducting an experiment. Or reclaiming the grass for his soccer-playing brethren. The ball bounces off the head of the guy and he decouples and looks at the boy, stunned. Before he can say anything, the boy picks up the ball and runs back to join his friends. The couple get up, mumbling to themselves about the injustice that has just been perpetrated upon them and leave. On the back of the woman, on her white t-shirt, a stain. It's brown and smeared over a large area just near her shoulder blades.

From a bench in the park, the laughter of a man who doesn't believe in fate. But who feels perhaps a lot better, if not cleansed.

SQUISHY

1

The smell of deep fried seafood is one of those things that makes me doubt my atheism. God may not be great but deep fried seafood most definitely is. The chemical composition of seared flesh, oil, bread crumbs. Exhaust. There's always exhaust because the best smells always emanate from buildings surrounded by copious parking.

The smell attracts crowds.

Here, on a quiet street in a kind of suburb south of Portland, Maine, the smell is so attractive the parking lot has been built especially large—even by the standards of American parking lots.

The building is essentially a white barn. Red mansard-style roof. Screened-in front porch. The parking lot surrounds two sides of the restaurant. A grass sward covers the far side. In front, a concrete patio with picnic tables and between it and the road, a grassy area interspersed with stunted evergreens. Across the street, a tidal flat that in most continents would be a malarial hive of hideous tropical fauna. Snakes. Fish that eat people. Vultures feeding on bulls killed by lizards. Here, in Maine, one can rent a canoe and go for a paddle. Graceful herons spear fish from the brackish water. Children paddle boat with tubby dads sporting the latest in pink and teal golf shirts.

The road leads, eventually, to the beach, as all roads in Maine must, to a sandy shore that would be perfect were it not for the Arctic temperatures of the waters. Swimming here is castration. I do not swim the ocean in Maine. Instead, I eat. Fried seafood mostly.

2

Ben Good struggles to understand what he knows he is about to witness. This in itself is new to him. At this juncture in his life, understanding has never been a problem. Confusion is to Ben Ernest Good what pork is to most people of Semitic extraction.

Yes, he is named after the famed clarinetist. His father played. His father toured the world as a jazz clarinetist before a series of unfortunate incidents led to his abandoning music. Ben's mother was a piano teacher. Mostly classical. His sister is lead violinist in a small regional symphony in Minnesota. The family is musical.

Ben is not. He is intelligent and slightly odd–but only in the socially odd way that intelligent people are–and lives a life that is free of cultural appreciation. He does not participate in or watch any kind of sport. He is fanatical about bridge. And despite specialized cable's insistence on the matter, no card games are sport. They are games.

Ben watches and struggles for words. He is unsure of how to react. His body leans back until he is supported by the window that overlooks a balcony overlooking a beach shaded by palms. The ocean beyond is the turquoise of, well, an ocean. It is a turquoise that has the possibility of announcing the beginning of life's denouement.

These are the some of the steps that led to Ben's predicament:
1) Ben is born.
2) Ben's eldest sister clubs him in the left leg with a croquet mallet.
3) Ben finds his father's "magic" clarinet in a closet. Ben breaks the clarinet.
4) Ben's best friend moves to Alberta.
5) Ben is hit in the face by a football thrown by an advertising executive who had once been the starting quarterback on his high school football team.

6) Ben's mother accidently clubs him in the left leg with a wooden meat tenderizer.

7) Ben discovers his father's porn stash hiding in the same closet as the now mythical "magic" clarinet.

Ben entered university at 16. He developed theories that made him a rising star in the world of theoretical physics. His awkward voice, with its uncertain timbre and unfortunate habit of cracking at the most serious moments disarmed colleagues and made them underestimate him. Until he put chalk to board. Until he created a series of equations that were the mathematical equivalent of a Boticelli. His work was enough to earn him standing ovations and cries of "Bravo!" at conferences the world over. At 22, he accepted a post at the University of Chicago, way station for physicists on their path to the glory that is Nobel.

He was still a virgin. He'd had no time for sex. At least that was his justification. Just the thought of it hurt his legs. Especially his left one.

3

The room is the kind of thing that reminds you of a minimum security prison. On your right, a dark waiting area and two bright red doors that lead to the lavatories. On your left, a small bar stocked with an entire shelf of cheap vodka. Below it, an array of emtpy beer bottles.

The room is long and bright. On the right hand wall, a series of sliding glass partitions separate the room from the kitchen. This is where you order your food. Above the windows, the menu, a list that once read leads to both intense desire and cardiac arrest.

On the opposite wall, windows out onto the picnic area and beyond it, the tidal flat. The tables covered in the red and white checked tablecloth that says informal, let the kids make a mess. Large communal type tables. Fried food that doesn't necessitate the use of utensils tastes better when eaten with strangers.

It is always full, this place. Almost all are tourists. Meaning they are not well-dressed. Adults who should not are wearing shorts. Old women. Fat men. Fat old men and women. I look up to the menu and begin what at this moment feels like the most important decision I have ever made.

4

Picture a bar where no one on the dance floor is in synch. As if they are dancing to different songs. And then you notice they are. Everybody is dancing to the tunes from their respective iPods. It's the Charlie Brown Christmas play but the kids are older and dress better. It's a funny kind of chaos. You watch not knowing whether to be fascinated or repulsed. This is mystification. Understand this at least.

It is what you feel watching the gradation of emotion on Ben E. Good's face.

Her name is Elizabeth Sweet. It would be. She is a graduate student from New Zealand. Three years ago she read Ben's paper on the possible malleability to the physical properties of certain forms of light in zero gravity. What got her was the poetry of the lead equation.

When she was 17, Elizabeth Sweet was voted Miss Teen Christchurch. She's a looker. With brains and an interest in physics. And ever since reading Ben's paper she has followed his career and, when possible, attended conferences where he was speaking. Like this one.

Unlike other conferences, she got to meet him this time. She found him on a leather couch in the lobby of the conference centre, waiting for a colleague to return with a bottle of water. She introduced herself. She took his hand in both of hers and asked him out to dinner. She mentioned the paper on zero gravity. Ben was hungry.

Some of the things Ben and Elizabeth discussed during their dinner:

1) The view. He was for, she was against.
2) A new theory posited out of Kazakhstan in the field of thermo-dynamics.
3) The politics of eating squid.
4) Mallets
5) Electromagnetics
6) Cellphones in restaurants. Both were against.
7) The green pants worn by the squid-eating middle-aged woman talking loudly into her cellphone at the next table.

Ben ordered conch fritters, an oyster salad and grilled octopus. Elizabeth took the spaghetti with clams and ordered a bottle of chardonnay. Ben was mildly amused by her. She flattered him. And she ate with an abandon that aroused in Ben... something. His confusion started when he saw her eat.

Ben doubted that he had ever even noticed how people ate but this woman in front of him attacked her dinner like a starving child suddenly finding itself in the midst of a storm where it rains apple pie.

Ben thought of saying something half witty, along the lines of the just declassified reports of the hungry women of New Zealand, but by the time his mouth started forming the words, they were gone, forgotten in the confusion that gripped him. He managed something monosyllabic. A grunt. He sounded like a horse the moment after a bug had flown up its nose.

5

This is what it comes to. A clam sandwich platter. Fries. And a small "appetizer" of fried lobster claws but only because I don't really think lobster should ever be fried but then again, I felt the same way about Twinkies and that turned out pretty good.

Decision made, I step up to one of the glass partitions and a teenage girl, probably a senior in high school, opens the glass. Her pencil awaits my command. I order. She writes it down and hooks the order to an aluminum wall–behind which more high school seniors deep-fry the bounty of the sea. She hands me a piece of paper where she has scribbled a number. 112. I pay. I leave a tip in a jar. "We'll call you when it's done, sir," she says. For once, I don't mind being called "sir." Not when the reward is a clam sandwich on a quiet road in coastal Maine.

I find a seat. I wait. I take in the air and can practically see the particles of oil floating around the place. It is a far more appealing sensory experience than the sight of the tourists in their shorts. Outside, children run among the stunted trees, their t-shirts announcing pit stops on their travels.

I close my eyes. The smell is something both industrial and primal.

The sun enters the restaurant. It lights up the glass partition and the activity behind it. Bivalves are unvalved. Crustaceans meet their maker. Fish guts fly into plastic tubs. And the oil. Always, the oil, glistening, golden, poured into giant vats like so much Turkish coffee.

"112," says a young voice over the loudspeaker. I stand. But before I do, I feel my body give in to something. It prepares itself for surrender. I am about to enter the temple. The womb of the matter. The deep-fried version of gustatory bliss. Because I can smell it. This is the rapture.

6

Elizabeth managed to get Ben to her room. Ben had heard about such things, especially at these conferences. He knew what was coming and he didn't mind. Except for the confusion. He liked the way she said certain words. These included "recumbent," "square," "Kuiper," "astonishing," and, mostly, "lovely." Her accent was the kind of refined / rough talk that always makes even the most educated New Zealander seem slightly loutish. He liked that. The accent seemed to remove the need for pretense.

At the end of the meal, she had simply said, "Alright then, are you going to come up to my room?" and he shrugged and she had taken his hand and led him out of the restaurant. In the elevator she said, "We've connected." She said, "I'm very happy right now." She also said, "Isn't this lovely?" And he shrugged and said, "I don't know," and his voice got all squeaky and she giggled and the doors of the elevator opened and she said, "It is, Ben." And before he could respond or even understand he was standing by her bed and she was on it. And she was unbuttoning her shirt.

Ben doesn't feel so good right now. He feels luck, in a strange sense, but not good. He is confused because

1) He doesn't believe in luck. He believes in probabilities but not luck.

2) He can feel the gravitational pull of Elizabeth's breasts.

3) He hates the irrationality of all of this.

4) What he hates even more is the fact that the sight of Elizabeth's breasts creates a flashback to his father's porn stash, creating a flashback to his father, creating a feeling of the deepest revulsion, adding to his confused state.

5) He is aroused.

6) He is very aroused.

7) Elizabeth is unzipping her skirt.

She shimmies out of the skirt. She shimmies out of her underwear. And now she is in front of Ben E. Good, exposed, naked, inviting him to taste something, a foreign world. Elizabeth Sweet is a doorway into a party that has never invited Ben. "Come over," she says.

Ben feels the cold of the window on his back. He wants to say something. He clears his throat. He takes a step forward. He feels as if he is watching this from somewhere else, disembodied, ironically, since he is very, painfully, aware of the erection pressing against his pants. She sits up now. She spreads her legs. She rubs herself and then spreads her lips and looks at him so deeply he feels commanded.

Ben is by the bed. He feels weakened. He falls to his knees. He sees where he must go. He knows what he must do. His mind can discern this even amidst the chaos. He leans forward. She takes his head. Instinctively, he opens his mouth. His tongue comes out. He closes his eyes. He smells something mysterious and feels his insides scream with pleasure. It is pleasure he feels. This much he understands. He leans forward some more until he's surrounded.

7

I go to the window. The girl hands me an orange tray. A pretense at slaw accompanies the clams. The clams overflow from the sandwich and the plate like some kind of lava. The lobster claws, shaped like blobs of breading. Deep-fried lobster is a dead crustacean that has been given an identity crisis. The obligatory slice of lemon. I get extra napkins. I fill three small paper cups with tartar sauce. I walk back to my seat. I open up the sandwich and spread tartar sauce over the clams. I squeeze the lemon over everything. Inhale. Remember pleasant things. Childhood. First home run. Losing my virginity. I eat a fry. To prep the palate. I close the sandwich.

I lift it off the plate. I open my mouth. My tongue comes out to grab the sandwich, like the tentacle of an octopus. I close my eyes. I can smell my sandwich, feel the heat of it, feel the sauce oozing onto my fingers and I lean into it until it's inside my mouth and I am lost and whole and something else altogether.

THE IDOLS

"I need jeans," Jack says, watching low res amateur porn on his laptop. He doesn't say this to anyone in the room; it's just an announcement.

"You need more than that," Angie says.

"Dude," Lulu says. "You always want something."

Jack closes his laptop. He walks over to his wallet and looks inside. "Bank," he says.

"Fuck the bank," Derek says.

Jack puts his wallet in his back pocket. He sighs, just to ensure that everyone in the room understands what he wants. And that he wants it now.

"I'll come with you," Angie says.

Lulu rolls over to Derek and kisses his arm. Derek blows smoke rings. He flips the page of his magazine. Because he's bored with the page. Just because. "Some pages have too many fuckin' words," he says. "And then some have none. Like fuckin' make up your mind."

Lulu licks Derek's arm. "Put it on plastic, asshole," she says.

Jack doesn't say anything. Nobody does. He makes for the door. Angie gets up. "Wait," she says. "I said I was coming."

"I like that," Jack says.

The smoke in the apartment is like the sky over Mexico during thermal inversion. Al walks out of the bathroom, his pants by his ankles. "My dick is itchy," he announces. "I gots itchy dick."

"Fuck off, that's gross," Lulu says.

"Fuck you," Al says.

Angie finds her purse under the table. "Like, what, 7 For All Mankind?" she asks. "True Religion?"

Jack shrugs. "I don't know. I'll see," he says. "I'm thinking old school."

"What's that mean?" Lulu asks. "Calvins? Do they even make jeans anymore?"

"No, like Levi's," Jack says. "Or Wranglers."

"I don't know you," Derek says.

"Maybe I'll buy something," Angie says.

"So go already," Lulu says.

"Pump up the economy," Al says. "Do something for the peeps."

Lulu squeezes Derek's crotch.

He puts out his cigarette. "Who has something to smoke?" he asks.

Al walks into a bedroom.

"I'm hungry," Lulu says. "For like sushi something."

"Sushi is so over," Angie says, putting on lipstick. "The Japanese kill whales. The whole Japanese thing is finished. *Domo arigato,* dude."

"There's no good sushi in this fuckin' city," Derek says. "Not that I care."

"I'm going," Jack says and then he doesn't move.

Angie stands up. "OK already," she says.

Jack and Angie walk outside and the sun assaults them like a perfectly thrown javelin. Angie sports a deep bronze but it's from a sun at least three thousand miles to the south. Jack hates tanning. He's selectively chemical free. He has the color of underdone French toast and wears his pale skin with pride. He likes that his lips are so red and the contrast this provides to his face. He's convinced this makes him sexy. Angie is on an airplane every second month. She plans her trips around the state of her tan. "Are we walking?" she asks.

"Shut up," Jack says.

Angie's father made his fortune as an Internet domain name squatter. He thought of one hundred nouns that might be lucrative in the future and he bought them with two friends. They bought the words in both single and plural forms. They made millions on "car." They had, at first, basic words like "pet" and "chair" and "stereo." He could retire before Angie was twelve. On her thirteenth birthday, he gave her ten nouns and she squatted on them until the idea of squatting was outlawed in the US. She sold them. To Europeans who continue to sit on common words like expectant hens. "Blue?" she asks.

"I don't know, stop asking so many fuckin' questions," Jack says.

"I like indigo more than blue," she says.

"Good," he says.

"Indigo's big in Brazil," she says.

Jack's family started up a Green food business, long before any-one had thought of a mass need for one. They opened a store that became a chain. And then they sold it. The family business has made Jack conscious of some things. He will not eat red meat unless he knows its provenance. Or poultry. He knows too much, he says. Or anything that isn't organic. He's thinking about giving up fish. He prefers raw food. Jack smokes and drinks to excess. He enjoys French biodynamic wines. His friends can't go out to dinner with him. Derek, in particular, mocks his diet every chance he gets. Derek is the opposite of Jack. Derek only eats steak.

Jack and Angie walk down the street as if lost. Their pace is glacial. Jack takes out a cigarette and Angie takes one from him. "Like you need jeans," she says.

"I didn't say I needed jeans," he says.

Angie's cellphone rings and she takes it out of her purse. "Lulu says they're going out for Chinese."

Jack lights his cigarette and offers the matches to Angie.

"What the fuck does it mean?" Al asks.

Derek sits up and puts his hand through his hair. "What, your dick?"

"It looks normal," Al says.

"I've seen your dick," Lulu says.

"Fuck off," Al says.

"Your pole," she says.

"Take a shower or something," Derek says.

"I'm serious," Al says.

"Your fuckstick," Lulu says.

Derek stands up and looks around, as if the answer is somewhere in the apartment. "Go to the fuckin' doctor," Derek says.

"My doctor is also my parents' doctor," Al says.

"What the fuck?" Derek says.

Lulu finds a cigarette and lights it. She stands up and walks to the window. "It's sunny," she says.

"My cock's itchy and you're telling me the weather?" Al asks. He puts his hands down his pants.

"Dude, that's fuckin' disgusting," Derek says. "Don't touch anything else."

"C'mon, I'm hungry," Lulu says. "I told Angie we were going for Chinese."

"You're going for Chinese," Derek says, correcting her.

Lulu turns around. "They'll have steak."

"They'll have beef," Derek says. "They don't have steak. The Chinese don't do steak. They'll have strips of overcooked beef."

"They have pork chops," Al says.

"Al, who are you talking to?" Derek says.

Al walks into the bathroom. "Take a fucking shower!" Derek says.

Lulu walks to Derek and sits on his lap. "You'll come?"

"I'll get a *mai tai* or something," he says.

Lulu kisses him. She opens her mouth and her tongue is licking his tonsils.

"Fuck!!!" Al screams in the bathroom.

Derek lies Lulu down on the floor.

Al's father is the president of a firm specializing in forensic accounting. He expects Al to study accounting as well. Al is avoiding confronting his father by studying accounting. He doesn't know what he wants but he understands that the button-down world of his father's firm is as relevant to him as Turkish cinema. Al wants to travel and figure things out. He wants to get his own place. He wants to spend a year on a beach somewhere doing nothing. Or as long as it takes until he figures out what he's going to do. "It burns when I piss!" he yells.

Derek's parents own a series of dog spas. Before that, Derek's father was a botanist. His mother owned a soap boutique. And then Derek's father read about a pet spa in California and he saw it. He saw the next big thing. He said, "pets are the new kids." And then he heard about a dog spa in Vancouver and he went there and studied it. He rented dogs in Vancouver so he could go to the spa every day. Derek didn't know you could rent a dog. It sounded sick to him. They pooled their savings, and borrowed from their families. Their dog spas have done very well and now they were franchising. His parents' weird business decisions had put money in his bank account. Who was he to judge? He had never enjoyed so much as a manicure. He once went to a spa in Antigua with Lulu and Angie and he drank rum the entire time. He remembers pouring rum into the open beak of a giant sea gull.

Lulu's father died while jogging. He was hit by a motorcycle at an intersection near their house. He left all his money to his children. He'd traded derivatives. She never understood what that meant. It sounded negative to her. Her parents were divorced. Because her father was sleeping with the Guatemalan maid. She hadn't heard from her mother in five years. And then her father died and her mother showed up at the funeral. It was her mother's idea to name her Lulu after the comic strip. She grew up being called Little Lulu. And when the will was read, her mother flew off in a rage and Lulu and her brothers hadn't heard from her since.

"I like the sound of Wranglers," Jack says.

"Whatever," Angie says.

"They sound cool," he says.

"Loser," Angie says.

"Who wears Wranglers?" Jack asks.

"Like who watches TV," Angie adds.

Jack asks the clerk if they sell Wranglers and the clerk stifles laughter. "I think we have some Lees," she says. "We might."

"So where can I get Wranglers, do you know?" Jack asks.

"Like a department store?" the clerk says, unsure of her answer. She's never been asked such a question.

"Oh, fuck, Jack, just buy something," Angie says.

Jack looks around the store. "No, really," he says.

The clerk just stares at him, willing him to leave. "Can I help you with anything else?" she asks.

"You do not talk like that," Angie says.

The clerk looks at the cash, stifling an urge. Her manager is within earshot. "I'm sure you can buy your jeans on the web or something," she says.

"I can't buy jeans on the fuckin' web," Jack says. "I need to try them on. I don't know how Wranglers fit."

"They fit like shit," Angie says. "Unless you're, like, a cowboy or a football player or something." She puts a piece of gum in her mouth. On her third chew she blows a bubble.

Jack stays at the cash staring at the clerk. "What else?" he asks.

"What else what?" the clerk asks.

Jack runs his hands through his hair. The clerk's cute but Angie's right behind him. "Can I special order?" he asks.

"I doubt we even know the phone number," the clerk says.

"Fuck," Jack says.

"You said it," the clerk says. She has a nose ring. And a spiky tentacle-like tattoo inching up her neck to her chin.

"I'll be back," he says.

"Is that a threat?" the clerk says. Angie laughs.

"That's not what I meant," Jack says. "Fuck." He feels flustered. The clerk notices how pale he is and finds it attractive. "I will," he says. "Let's go," he says to Angie.

They leave but as they do, Jack turns around to see the clerk watching him. She smiles.

"Drugs," Al says.

"Meth, hash and coke," Derek says.

"I mean I need drugs for my dick," Al says.

"Fuck your dick," Lulu says.

"And some pot somewhere," Derek says.

"What would McGyver do with an itchy dick?" Al asks.

"There's gotta be a website for your stupid problem," Lulu says.

Derek reaches into his pocket and pulls out a small tin box. He opens it and studies its contents. "And some speed," he says.

"Roll a joint," Al says.

"C'mon, I'm really hungry," Lulu says. She walks to the kitchen and finds nothing but a bag of organic chips. "Jack doesn't eat," she says.

Derek burns some hash and rips up a cigarette and drops some coke on the whole thing.

"What are we doing?" Al says squirming.

"Let's do this first," Derek says.

Lulu returns to the room. "Stale chips," she says.

Derek licks the joint and lights it. He takes three deep puffs and hands it to Al. "Cheers," he says.

Al takes three quick puffs and inhales deeply. He gives Lulu the joint. "I'm hungry," she says again.

"Bitch, you'll be hungrier," Derek says.

Al laughs.

"I'm serious," Lulu says giving Derek the joint.

"So am I," he says, and he takes a long drag.

The doorbell rings. "Crap," Lulu says.

"See who it is," Al says.

Lulu gets up. "It's not like he has a peeper or whatever they're called," she says.

"Just ask," Derek says.

"It must fucking stink in here," Al says.

Lulu tiptoes to the door. She clears her throat. "Who is it?" she asks.

"It's Sam," comes the voice from the other side.

Lulu opens the door. Sam enters, Jack's older brother. He inhales deeply. "What is that?" he asks, smiling.

"You want some," Derek says, holding out the joint.

"You guys are so Less Than Zero," Sam says. He walks to Derek and takes the joint.

"I have no idea what that means," Derek says staring at Sam. "But it sounds gay."

Sam takes a puff. "What's inside this?" he asks.

"Love," Derek says.

Sam coughs. "No really, what is this shit?" he asks.

"Whatever I found," Derek says.

Sam gives the joint to Al. "Where's my brother?" he asks, his voice raw.

"He said he needed jeans," Lulu says.

"He doesn't need jeans," Sam says.

Al squirms. His crotch feels like it's on fire. He can only imagine what the problem is. He passes the joint to Lulu. She hands it straight to Derek.

"He said jeans, right?" Lulu says.

Derek shrugs and sucks on the joint and then puts it out in the ashtray. He lights a cigarette.

"I'm sure he said jeans," Lulu says.

Sam sits on the couch. "It's a nice day outside," he says.

"Where did you go last month?" Derek asks Lulu.

"Cabo," she says.

"I'd like to go there," he says.

"Is he gone for long?" Sam asks.

"Who?" Derek asks.

"Jack," Sam says.

"Fuck if I know," Derek says.

Lulu lies down. She reaches up for Derek's cigarette. "Get your own," he says.

Al gets up and goes to the bathroom.

"He hates shopping," Sam says.

Derek shrugs.

"He likes jeans," Lulu says.

Sam sighs. "Jeans are a racket."

"You're wearing jeans," Lulu says.

"And they're fuckin' gay," Derek says.

"You like saying that," Sam sighs.

Lulu laughs.

"What's wrong with my jeans?" Sam asks.

"You don't mean that," Derek says.

"What?" Sam asks. "They cost too little?"

Derek shrugs.

"That I can't imagine paying more than sixty bucks for my jeans?" Sam says. "They're, what, too wide? Fuck this whole slim thing. It's a once-a-decade thing. Half the world looks stupid in them. Once every ten years, the designers get together in their star chamber and decide to go skinny again. It lasts two years. And then it's back to the regular jeans. Boot cuts. Straight legs. Whatever. But meanwhile, you've spent thousands of dollars on slim jeans."

"Can openers," Derek sniffs. He puts out his cigarette.

"1978. 1984. 1996," Sam says. "Skinny jean years. I'm wrong about the dates, probably. But it's once a decade." He sighs. "What was in that fuckin' joint?" he asks.

Lulu giggles. She sits up and finds a cigarette and takes Derek's still burning stub out of the ashtray to light hers.

"The younger generation swings," Sam says.

"You're, like, from another planet," Derek says.

"The brother from another planet," Sam says.

"I don't know what that means, dude," Derek says.

The room is silent. The toilet flushes and Al walks in. He looks panicked. "I gotta go," he says.

"You just did," Derek says. Lulu laughs at this.

Sam looks at Al. "What's wrong?" he asks.

Al says nothing. "I just gotta go," he says.

"His dick's itchy," Derek says.

Sam looks at Al to see if perhaps this is the truth.

Al goes to the kitchen and drinks water from the tap.

"For real?" Sam calls.

"I gotta go," Al says again. He checks his pockets for his wallet, his keys and his cell and he leaves.

"Don't say bye or nothing," Lulu says, laughing some more. "Fuckwad."

"Levi's are fine, I guess," Jack says. He and Angie walk down the street, smoking. "They just don't mean the same thing. They don't mean anything."

"They're Boomer jeans," Angie says. "Levi's are like, you know your size, they always fit. Dependable. They can try and cool them up but they're always Levi's and they'll always be Boomer jeans."

"Really?" Jack says.

"Whatever," Angie says.

"My brother wears Levi's," Jack says.

"Then he's a Boomer wannabe," she says.

"He's going to think that sucks," Jack says.

"It's over for him," she says.

"I'll stick to Wranglers," he says.

"You're not making a statement, fuck," she says. "You might as well wear, like, Dockers or something."

"Take that back," Jack says.

"What's the point of jeans then?" she asks.

"I think Levi's make Dockers," Jack says.

"I'm not so dumb," Angie says.

"The Wranglers will be awesome," he says.

They pass an art supply shop, a dressmaker, a pastry shop, an Indian restaurant. "What kind of department store?" Jack asks.

"I need a dress or something," Angie says.

They cross the street and pass by a mother pushing a baby in a carriage. Angie puts her cigarette behind her back. They walk toward the sun, setting now, almost, or threatening to. "If it's too hard I'm not going to do it," Jack says.

"It's too hard," Angie says.

A bicyclist in full biking gear, with skinny legs, his feet clipped into the pedals, his hairless legs the shape of twigs, zooms past, yelling at the driver of a red K class Mercedes.

"Asshole," Angie says.

"What else?" Jack says.

Angie's cellphone rings and she reaches into her purse. "Your brother's at your place," she says. "Derek rolled a joint."

Jack takes out his cellphone and calls his apartment. "Give it to Sam," he says. "No," he says. "I don't know, just give the fucking phone to my brother." Jack stops walking. "What's up?" he asks. He starts walking again.

"Black," Angie says. "Or, I don't know."

"Not a clue," Jack says.

"Shoes," Angie says.

"That's fucking ridiculous," Jack says.

"Shoes or a dress?" Angie says.

Jack listens to his brother on the phone. "Would you shut up?" he says to Angie. "Nothing," he says.

"Stop," Angie says and she walks into a small boutique with black dresses in the window. Jack follows her inside and sits on a large orange faux leather ottoman in the middle of the store.

"I don't know," Jack says. "Maybe."

He puts the phone back into his pocket. Angie holds up a black dress in front of her and looks into a floor length mirror. She frowns. "So?"

"I'm supposed to have lunch with my parents tomorrow," he says.

"No, stupid, the dress," she says.

He shrugs. "It's nice," he says.

"No it's not," she says.

"Then don't ask me," he says.

She puts the dress back and takes another one off the rack. She holds it in front of her and looks in the mirror. "I'm going to try this one," she says.

"Fuck off," Jack says. "We'll be here forever."

Angie runs off to the changing room. Jack looks deep into his cellphone unsure of what to do next. He wants to buy the jeans but the world is conspiring against his desires. It's not supposed to. If he could, he'd get angry about it.

Sam pours vodka into three shot glasses and walks them back to the room. Derek sits up. Lulu sits on her knees. Sam puts the glasses down on the table and sits on the couch. "OK?" he says.

They grab their shot glasses and clink them. And then they swallow the vodka and bring the glasses down on the table. "Where's the bottle?" Derek asks.

"Your turn," Sam says.

Lulu stretches her neck, her head doing graceful circles. Derek returns with the bottle. "Belvedere is like too good to do shots with," he says.

"Belvedere is the perfect thing to do shots with," Sam says.

Lulu laughs. Derek pours the vodka in to the three glasses. "So," he says.

They pick them up and shoot the drinks down. Lulu gags and Derek is refilling the glasses.

"Wait," Lulu says.

"This is my last one," Sam says. "And then I'm out."

"Stay a while," Derek says.

"I'm supposed to take the kids to the park," Sam says.

He takes his glass and downs his shot and stands. "Great," he says. "Don't waste the whole day inside. It's nice outside." He walks to the door and leaves.

Derek does his shot. "Let's go," he says.

"Where?" Lulu asks.

"Drink up," he says.

"Wait," she says.

He lights a cigarette and pours himself another vodka. Lulu takes her glass and bends her head back and the drink is gone. Derek refills her glass and then refills his.

Lulu coughs. "Shit," she says. She giggles.

"Sam's cool," Derek says.

"Sam is a different kind of cool," Lulu says. "Like an older cool." She takes her shot glass and stares at it. "He's cool like sometimes you see an old show on TV and they're wearing something totally hip but it's just kind of wrong. Like the actress is just a bit... heavy. He's like that."

"One, two, three," Derek says and he picks up his glass and the vodka is gone. He takes a deep drag of his cigarette.

"He's like a total adult or something," Lulu says. She drinks her vodka. She places the shot glass upside down on the table. She leans back and almost falls over. She stumbles again and then gives in to gravity and lies down. She closes her eyes.

"He's got cute kids," Derek says, staring at the ceiling.

"Yeah, I don't get that," she says.

"Get what?" he says.

"Kids," she says.

A deep kind of liquid sound comes out of Lulu. Derek looks at her and takes a drag of his cigarette. "We need music," he says.

The sound comes from her again. Derek finds Jack's iPod and hooks it up to the stereo. A riff, a beat, a wail. Derek turns up the volume.

Angie doesn't buy the dress, which doesn't surprise Jack. "Let's go," he says.

"I liked that dress," she says. "It didn't fit right. Fuckin' tits." She grabs both her breasts and squeezes.

Jack walks toward the door and Angie catches up and they step into the sunshine and light cigarettes. "Let's go home," he says.

"They're having Chinese," Angie says.

"Derek's not eating Chinese," Jack says.

"Fuck," Angie says.

"Let's go," Jack says. "We'll order in or something."

"You don't order in," she says.

"There's a place that I order from," he says. "I'll order from there. Lulu can get her fuckin' Chinese. Derek'll probably go out and get a steak and barbecue it or something and make one of his creamy pepper sauces or something. You do what you want."

They walk toward his apartment, oblivious. A police car screams down the street. Angie looks in the window of every boutique that might have a dress. Jack takes her hand and pulls her away when she changes course and threatens to enter one of them.

"You're mean," she says.

"I'll buy you a dress," he says. "I'll buy you a fuckin' dress tomorrow. Or something."

She laughs. "Cool," she says.

"Fine," he says.

They walk in silence back to his apartment. They find Derek dancing in front of the stereo. His eyes are closed and he bobs his head to the beat. Lulu lies on the floor, her face the color of used Astroturf. Jack and Angie walk into the bedroom and undress.

SMART MEN DO DUMB THINGS

When Pink Floyd's "One Of These Days" comes on the radio, Rob decides he's had enough. An hour of music written way before he was born. The Rolling Stones. Cream. Pink Floyd. The Byrds. He sees the evolution of the radio as something sinister, a technology in its death throes, the last refuge of a decaying and annoying generation, but for now, he's wishing he had listened to his friends and invested in satellite. He hates the radio.

The scenery on this drive is unspectacular. The fact that the road between Montreal and Toronto is so boring, among the most boring in the world, must mean something. It must say something about Canada that this road, connecting its two largest cities, is full of nothing. Sporadic forests give way to tumble-down barns fronting the flatness of agriculture. The monotony of the colours by the side of the road. Speeding past a featureless nothingness. The country's supposed heartland. There's a lake and river close by but you'd never know it. The road is made for efficiency, not beauty. Rob's New York friends always complain about the New Jersey Turnpike, but they don't know the 401. A friend in Chicago who works in furniture has to drive a triangle between Milwaukee and Des Moines every month and perhaps he would understand the utter banality of the road between Montreal and Toronto. But to Rob, the road is more than just boring, it is a national scandal. Or something. Rob speeds by the giant apple, unaware of the great pies inside.

He spent two days in Toronto trying to reconnect with an old girlfriend and that went nowhere. She's pleased with the move. She has the job she thinks will fulfill her, in PR. Rob doesn't understand PR and doesn't understand her happiness and when he realized this he gave up. Her new mood was enough to kill his old mood. He wanted to be happy, too, and he couldn't do it with someone who was happy in Toronto, in PR.

Rob walks up the stairs up to his condo and decides, OK, that's that. Let's get a move on. He cleans out his mailbox and checks his phone messages and then calls Lou and asks if he wants to go out for a drink. He needs a drink, he says. He needs a drink and to talk about nothing while sounding vaguely profound.

"What is it about the radio?" Rob asks Lou.

"Montreal has the crappiest radio," Lou says. "It's like the last bastion of crappy radio. Even the jazz station plays crap. The rock station plays classic rock, which someone will figure out is a crock one of these days. It's the crock station. There's so much talk radio in this city, in two languages. And classical. Get into a cab and it's like you've walked into the drawing room in some sepia toned BBC production."

"My last cab driver was in a band," Rob says. "So I tell him to put on his own music, if he has it, and he does. He hooks it up and it was awesome. I'm sure they're some *band*, you know, someone I should know about, everyone's in a band, and they're all getting deals. I just don't think you make any money selling music anymore."

"You have to perform," Lou says.

"You have to perform," Rob says. "You have to go out and play and play and get on the road and play in Buttfuck, Ontario, and then you make some money."

"It's so Montreal that there's music everywhere just when there's no industry left," Lou says.

Rob finishes his beer and orders another. Lou nurses his pint. And then orders two rounds of tequila shots. "So?" he asks.

"She's in PR," Rob says.

"Is that bad?" Lou says.

Rob shrugs. "Not really. Sort of. She's way too happy in it. She loves that stuff. She's happy."

"Happiness is alright," Lou says. "It can make life easier."

"Sure," Rob says. "I don't begrudge her happiness. I just realized I can't be happy with her. I went on a fishing trip. I caught nothing. We're different people now."

The waitress returns with Rob's beer and the tequila. A wedge of lime perched on each shooter. She puts a salt-shaker on the table and leaves. "She's cute," Lou says.

"She goes out with the owner," Rob says.

"That doesn't mean she's not cute," Lou says.

They perform the tequila ritual. They down their shots. Rob dislikes tequila and wonders every time why he bothers. "That ain't Patrón," he says. He grabs his beer and drinks.

"So are you going to move on?" Lou asks.

"I've moved on," Rob says.

"That's it?"

"That's it."

"No more?"

"That's it," Rob says.

"Great," Lou says. "I'm happy. It took long enough."

Rob thinks about this and realizes for the first time that he had allowed this breakup to last too long. He understood, while in Toronto, that the trip itself was a sign of confusion, or loss, or a combination. He hadn't thought it pathetic. Though now he was thinking perhaps it was. "It's time to reconnect," he says. "I'm moving on."

Lou taps his friend's arm. "At last," he says.

This is the thing about the radio. You grow up and you listen and it's fine, it's playing the music that's out. New albums come out and it gets on the radio. And then, suddenly, the radio isn't playing new albums anymore. Record stores close. Rock radio becomes "classic" and everyone gets their music off the Internet. No one watches videos anymore, the technology settles into what it really is: an ad. Friends start hyping satellite. The radio station has the same audience it had forty years ago except that audience is forty years older. What happens when the audience starts dying off? Have the radio geniuses thought that far ahead? Maybe they can take some notes from the opera folk. Or the classical folk. Soon, the three demographics will be the same. Add jazz. Rock, opera, classical, jazz. Make a station with all four and you have a great place to capture that audience for advertisers. Like funeral homes. Or reverse mortgages. Or old-age insurance packages. It's all very depressing.

Rob thinks this as he walks to a Portuguese chicken place to meet André. The air here is smoky with the grilled chicken-flesh of a half dozen Portuguese restaurants. André is sitting at the window and waves Rob in. "How are you, my friend?" he asks, extending his hand, taking Rob's, shaking it warmly. André's face is perfectly round. The man likes to eat. His breasts stretch his t-shirt to its limits. His hair is thinning. His jeans fall down his ass.

"I'm hungry," Rob says, smiling.

"I heard you were in Toronto?" André says.

"I went, I saw, I returned," Rob says.

"C'est terminé?" André asks, studying his friend's face. For a sign that he's lying.

"It's finished, yes," Rob says. "Yes! Let's not talk about it."

André laughs. "This happened to me once," he says. "I had a blonde, Sophie, remember her? Really nice. Really cool. We lived together, and then, suddenly, just like that, she leaves. She met some guy from *Laval* at a bar on Saint Laurent and that's it. She moves to Laval. Well, I couldn't lose her to some asshole from Laval. From

Laval! I was totally fucked by this. By her leaving me and because he was from *Laval.* I tried. I went out. I got some stupid *poupoune* from a bar and we went out for a week. But there was a song, a stupid song by a stupid singer, and she must have been big because I saw her on TV and I heard the song everywhere. Everywhere you went, that fucking song. It drove me crazy. It reminded me of Sophie. She sang it once, just once, in the shower. Just before she left me. So I went to Laval. I found out where she was and I went up to some shitty part of Laval, to this street with these boring duplexes, streets and streets of them, and when he opened the door, I lost it. I saw how small and fragile he was. Him! He was short and a bit fat and he shocked me, and I pretended I was going door-to-door selling mints for leukemia. And he asked to see my card. I didn't even know they had these cards, like identification, to prove you're not a crook. I don't know. I didn't know such a thing existed. I didn't even have any candy with me. He kicked me out and I was OK. I told myself I'll never do that again. When something's finished, it's finished. It was undignified what I did. I went to a movie in a mall up in Laval and then I ate a hamburger, I think I had a hamburger, and that was it. It was over."

Rob has no idea why André is telling him this but it comforts him to know that smart men do dumb things, and then he realizes why André has told him the story. "I felt similar except she doesn't have a boyfriend yet, just a new job."

"You're right, let's not talk about it," André says. "Enough. Let's look forward to the future."

Rob takes his napkin and spreads it on his lap. A waiter comes, a heavyset Portuguese man with a shirt unbuttoned low enough to unleash a tuft of thick black chest hair for everyone's viewing pleasure. *"Deux spéciaux,"* André says. *"Et une bouteille de vin, blanc, le vinho verde."*

"He smells," Rob says, holding his nose.

"Don't be a snob," André says.

"I prefer my waiters not to smell," Rob says. "I prefer my waiters on the clean side."

"Smell does not mean not clean," André says, something Rob finds ridiculous. "I come here all the time. It is my place. The food is always good. That waiter tends to smell, it's true. I think it's his clothes. Maybe they don't pay him enough to wash, I don't know. It's not really a problem, right? The food is good!"

André has been Rob's friend long enough to know when Rob needs his friendship. They are not close, they hardly see each other, but in a pinch Rob is sure André would do anything for him. He knows he would do anything for André. They've known each other too long, have told each other too much, to do otherwise. "So did you just want to have lunch or is there a reason?" Rob asks.

André feigns indignation. "Do we need a reason to enjoy lunch together?"

"No," Rob smiles. "But the message was so forceful. 'Meet me for lunch tomorrow. Don't say no.' It just sounded more important." Rob knows why André called him. He knows that André was concerned about his trip to Toronto, about the reclamation project. He was calling to check up, got voice mail, and suggested lunch instead.

"I only offer the pleasure of my company," André says.

"I can smell the waiter," Rob says.

"He's coming with the wine," André says. "And here he is."

That night, tired from an overlong lunch with André and with a headache after two bottles of the *vinho verde,* Rob lies on the couch. He finds a hockey game on TV and falls asleep. He dreams of a black and white world where the men smoked endlessly and the women wore pearls and cocktail parties lasted all night and everyone drove big cars. He saw himself, his hair slicked back, a rye in hand, debating the merits of Miles Davis. And when he wakes up, the late night sports anchor yells at him from the safety of his television studio, and Rob is disoriented and stumbles off the couch, rubbing the sleep from his eyes. He steps onto the remote control and the channel changes and he comes upon a Pink Floyd concert, except that it's not really Pink Floyd, it's the guys who call themselves Pink Floyd now, and they are playing on an elaborate stage in front of a grey haired multitude in a giant stadium. And then the concert breaks away to a lady who says, "If you love Pink Floyd, and who doesn't, then you'll see the need to support the great programming options on this public station...." and he steps on the remote again, and it's another episode of *Seinfeld,* an old one, the Chinese restaurant episode, and he walks to the kitchen and opens the pantry and takes out a bag of barbecue chips. He looks at the clock. It's one in the morning. He walks around his house and every light is on, the place hums, it throbs with a kind of invisible life and he feels alone. He lies back on the couch, his arm reaching into the bag of chips. He picks up the remote and wonders what song this version of Pink Floyd will play next. His money is on "Money."

THE DEFEATED

Claire was a beautiful woman. There was no denying that. And when she returned my flirtations in the bar down the street from my work, the bar the guys always call a "meat market" but which rarely if ever produced actual couplings, I worked up the courage to ask her out and she said yes. And this was an incredible thing to me because Claire was the kind of beautiful that I think most guys find intimidating. I was so comfortable with her that I took a dump in her place on our second date. Most women don't realize this but that's a very positive sign. It is the sign of impending commitment. It speaks to a level of intimacy that goes far beyond casual full frontal. And then there was this: Claire was more beautiful naked. Some girls aren't. Some girls are sexier with their clothes on. But with Claire, no, the less she wore the sexier she got. She got more beautiful. I realized this the first time we were involved in more than heavy petting. This was our third date. But this was also our last good date. Because this was the date I saw Claire's feet.

They were beyond ugly. It was as if her DNA had used itself up everywhere else and just let the feet go. Her feet looked like the chicken feet you let pass at *dim sum*. Her toes were like the runners in that Monty Python sketch about the 100 metre dash for people with no sense of direction. Feet can be many shapes but hers were a strange combination of round and hexagon. They were the shape of a badly cut t-bone. And I couldn't get them out of my head.

I am not superficial.

I am also not perfect. I hate myself more than anyone else.

After the date, I tried to put her feet out of my mind. I would concentrate on the perfectly round orbs that were her breasts, the loveliness of her belly button, the delicate curves of her shoulders, the smoothness of her thighs. Her sweet smell. The way her dark brown hair caressed her soft, soft back. But always, I came back to her feet.

After the third date, a colleague noticed me staring into nothing-ness at work and said, "you're in love."

"If only," I said.

"You're in lust," he said.

"It's not that simple," I replied.

"You're in lust with a girl you're in love with," he said.

I got up and went to the coffee machine.

I image searched "ugly feet" on Google and learned something about fetishes I hadn't ever imagined but did not find a photo of healthy feet that were remotely as ugly as Claire's. I saw photos of hideously deformed feet, and amputations, the feet of accident victims, and one gruesome shot of a baby's foot after it had been mauled by a pit bull. Claire's feet were healthy as far as I could tell. And I asked myself if I would have been more forgiving had her feet been unhealthy, had they been diseased or mutilated, had she perhaps once suffered frostbite while mountain hiking and lost three toes or had been the victim of an attack by sledgehammer.

Then there were the photos of the bound feet from China. Holy crap! What culture could possibly see those feet as anything other than what they were? The Chinese are completely crazy. I can't square their food–which is, for the most part, one of the great pleasures of life–and their history. And then the bound feet. Claire's feet didn't look bound, not at all. If anything, they were *unbound*. They were the opposite. They were feet that did not understand limits, or even the normal physical properties of feet. They were feet that had ignored the philosophical meaning of feetness.

I could not remember what kind of shoes Claire wore the first time I saw her.

I did not call her for two days. She left messages on my voice mail, each message a touch sadder. Finally, this: "Have I done something wrong?" And she hadn't, of course. Except that she had exposed her feet to me and I had recoiled so much that I was still moving backwards, as if I had been shot by a cannonball while in outer space. Would you ever stop floating backwards from such a strike? Or would you at some point get caught by the gravitational pull of a larger object and then eventually find yourself recoiling forward, with the cannonball still lodged in your belly? Or would you get hit by a comet at some point? I don't know, but the sheer ugliness of Claire's feet made me think such things.

And thinking this I figured it was me. And that I must have really loved Claire, already, to be so hung up on this imperfection, however major it was.

After all, hadn't I taken a shit in her toilet? Didn't that count for something?

And when I mentioned this to a friend on the phone, he understood. Amazingly. He said, I get this. He said, you know we all want that perfect woman but there's no such thing but when they get close, it hurts all the more. He said, it's like we all want gorgeous women who love to give porn star blow jobs and talk sports and eat like pigs but never gain weight and be smart and funny and have non-threatening careers and be so sexy it makes us hurt. He said, and then when we find out they know a bit too much about, say, hockey, like more than us, we start obsessing on that one mole on their neck, or how their blow jobs aren't quite good enough or who maybe aren't one hundred percent perfect, like maybe they have one inverted nipple. He said, and we just gloss over our own imperfections, of course. Because we're guys, he said. And, as guys, we aren't easy to live with. He said, we give ourselves a hard time. He said, basically we hate ourselves. It's why the world's so fucked. My friend's girlfriend is average looking. She's nice and all but I could see her for a full year before noticing she'd changed the colour of her hair.

I did the guy thing and avoided Claire's calls. Thank god for call display. I told myself, tomorrow. I'll answer tomorrow and, well, tomorrow's always a day away. If I didn't loathe myself before, and I'm sure I didn't, I was close to loathing myself now. Very, very close.

Is calling a guy a Neanderthal fair to Neanderthals? Apparently, they were smart and even sensitive–they buried their dead with flowers–and not a bunch of lumbering club-happy dolts. No. That would be us. Homo sapiens. We knew how to kill better. We were club-happy. I asked myself these things when my sister, upon hearing of my dilemma, which I told her, which maybe wasn't very smart, called me, among other things, an asshole, a boor, a fuckhead, an idiot, so fuckin' stupid, a loser, a jerk, a complete moron, a jerk-off, a fuck-up, a creep, a fuckin' stupid jack-off and a Neanderthal. And upon hearing all this, I could only think of how much we've impugned the reputation of those poor evolutionary dead ends. We're sore winners.

And my sister was right about everything even the Neanderthal thing in the sense of its widely accepted meaning.

The next day I called Claire. I apologized and told her I thought I was falling in love but had this one problem that I was ashamed to even think about. She said we should meet. I said no. We needed to talk but not face-to-face.

"Why?" she asked.

"I'm embarrassed to say," I said.

"Are you breaking up with me?" she asked. "Because I'm not even sure we had started to really go out, you know? But I thought we were a match and that good things would happen and that maybe we even had a future. I thought about the future."

I didn't say anything because everything she had said was true and because I tend to clam up when the conversation gets difficult. Especially with women.

"I've been trying to think about anything I've said or done," she said. She sighed. "I really like you. I want to make this work. I think it can. But I need you to tell me what's wrong. I need you to be honest. Without honesty, we have nothing."

I wanted to say, it's not you, it's me. I wanted to say, well, it's kind of... you, have you seen your feet lately? I wanted to tell her we could really make this work if she never took off her socks. I wanted to say, no, it's me, it really is and I can't explain it but that's the truth and I'm sorry to hurt you. Things that might have given me brownie points had I really deserved them but what guy does in the end?

"Claire, you're beautiful," I said.

It sounded as if something got caught in her throat.

"And I think I'm falling in love you," I said. "I don't know. Maybe I'm just afraid." And I wanted to say something resembling the truth.

"Afraid of what?" she asked.

"I'm afraid of being happy," I said. This resembled the truth somewhat though perhaps it was out of context.

"I can help you," she said. "I want to make this work."

"I'm not who you think I am," I said, sounding like, what. International man of mystery. How could I ever admit anything? I was a fraud but this did not really bother me so much.

I could hear Claire walking around her apartment. On her feet. "What does that mean?" she asked. "I think I have a good handle on you. I know you're not a bad person. You're a decent man. You make me laugh. The sex was good." A pause. "Wasn't it?"

The sex was OK but I wasn't going to complain. Guys in the end don't complain about sex. And definitely not about sex with a woman as beautiful as Claire. "It has nothing to do with sex," I said.

"Can I see you?" she asked. Her voice was trembling now which appealed to me in a kind of sick way. Her vulnerability made me horny.

"I don't know," I said. "I need time."

Another sigh. I should be honest with her, I thought. I should just say it, I thought. I liked her enough to be honest, to commit to an honest discussion if I was going to break up with her. I wanted to say the word "feet." Saying it would make everything easier. If I could somehow work the word into this conversation it could open things up. I would need to get it over with and then see if I couldn't move forward. Maybe honesty was a way of saving everything, a door to prosperity.

"I can't believe how much I've fallen for you after just a few dates," she said. "I usually don't fall for anyone quickly. I've always been so careful about opening up to guys. But you managed it. That's quite a feat." I almost dropped the phone.

"It is," I stammered, trying to respond properly.

"You're special," she said. "I really believe that."

"Why are you telling me this?" I said.

"Can we just meet and talk?" she asked. "I can come over. I miss you."

"I was honest about falling in love with you," I said. And I was. I wanted to yell the word "feet" at that moment. I wanted to yell it and feel better about things. How did she get those feet into a pair of shoes? I couldn't figure it out. I felt helpless. I felt lost in the loneliest place in the world. I felt like every single word my sister had called me, all of them. Even Neanderthal.

"I'm free right now," she said.

What was I going to say? I couldn't have sex with this woman anymore. She was beautiful. I had never bedded anyone as beautiful as her. I could see us arm in arm walking down the street and the other guys looking at me with an envy bordering on disgust. What guy doesn't want that feeling? What guy doesn't want to be *that* guy? If I couldn't be honest, what kind of future did we have? I sighed. I rubbed my hand through my hair. I checked my watch. I was going to find some sort of mental exercise to help me get over this. I was never going to play footsie. I would develop some kind of foot phobia just for her. A quirk that she would accept because she was a woman and women are more accepting.

"Please," she said.

"Come over," I said. I felt hollow almost. Empty. "We can work our way past this."

Claire is a beautiful woman.

CHICKEN SCRATCH

Even by the dusty standards of India, this is a dusty place. The air is thick with it. Streetlights are rendered impotent. Dust coats the buildings, the sidewalks, the cars and taxis and auto rickshaws. It is a feature of Dehra Dun and you get this before you even breath in the air.

The bus pulls into an empty plaza and sighs. It's midnight. I've just come from Delhi. Eight hours. My bones ache.

The driver opens the door and the dust rushes in. I stand and reach in the overhead for my backpack. I wait. The front half of the bus is crammed with families overburdened by a factory's worth of home electronics purchased in the city.

Whatever I came to find in India is not going to be found here. And one does embark on this sort of journey to find something. It is expected of you.

The town is unremarkable save for its botanical institute and an exclusive private school. How much must parents abhor their children to send them to a place like this? The Gandhi boys went to school here. From what I've read, the locals are proud of that. I step off the bus, take in the surroundings and open my *Lonely Planet*. The town rates less than a page: Dehra Dun, gateway to the Himalayan foothills–though in these parts, a foothill is a mountain anywhere else.

Scrawny chickens are everywhere, pecking at the gravel on the dusty roads. The plaza is surrounded by small tin-shack restaurants advertising tandoori chicken, the smoke from the ovens a low-lying haze, a commingling with the other particulates. I can only imagine the disease here. The lungs of the people.

I make out a hotel sign down a side street. Behind a ratty-looking door is a flight of brightly lit stairs painted what I've taken to calling "Krishna blue." The distorted sounds of a television fill the stairwell. All I ask of this hotel is basic cleanliness. And a lack of smells.

I could use a beer.

At the top of the stairs, a man with a round face and simple expression stares intently at the TV. An actress lip-synchs to a voice that is just this side of chipmunk. She dashes from tree to tree, coyly hiding from a flaccid-looking hero type with '70s porn star moustache. I have just described a scene from every Bollywood production that has enthralled this crazy, complicated nation. The actress has finished singing and now the actor gets overly emotive as he lip-synchs his lines. The innkeeper turns to me and smiles. A large, friendly smile.

"No more room," he says, his head doing that comical headshake Indians do to affirm the negative.

I drop my backpack. "I'm tired," I say, by way of explanation.

"No room." The innkeeper waves his hand in the general direction of my face. "And no English," he says.

"I just got off the bus and I need a bed. Anything you have. A bench. I'm tired. Please."

"Bed," he says. He points to a cot in the hallway behind me. "Light off. No problem." And with this he smiles some more, generally pleased to have offered me something.

The actress starts lip-synching again and I've lost him. "Ah hah hah," he says, closing his eyes rapturously. His head bobs to the tune like paper caught in a gentle breeze.

I walk to the cot—that's what it is, a cot—and sit. "I'll take it," I say. The innkeeper is lost in his Bollywood reverie. "I'll take it," I say a little louder. Nothing. His fingers drum the desk. He's playing *tabla,* accompanying the chipmunk voice and the synthetic drone of the music, dreaming of a world where he always gets the girl. "I'll take the damned cot!" I yell.

A door opens across the hall. A distinguished-looking older man in a beige safari suit eyes me. His thick white hair and white moustache show signs of obsessive grooming. He was a professor of some sort, at some time. Retired now. "Why would one sleep in a cot?" he asks in an English that hints at a British education. He is a kind of cliché but in India there are so many more clichés because there as so many more people.

I look at him dumbly. I don't know if I have it in me to answer him. The bus, the bumps and turns and sheer length of the ordeal have rendered me helpless.

"I know of a double room occupied by a young university boy," the old man says, raising his eyebrows. "Does this interest you?"

Before I can answer he has rushed down the hall and knocked on a door. The innkeeper runs after him. The door opens and the two men disappear inside. "He will fix you up," says yet another man who appears in the doorway of the old man's room. "He knows these things, yes?" This man is younger, with a foppish Beatles haircut, and a bushy moustache. He's tall and thin and swarthy. He looks like a man that might be hard to trust. "You will have no problems." He picks at his teeth with a well-used toothpick.

"Actually, I'd just like a beer," I say. "I'd settle for a pop."

"We can do better," the swarthy man says cryptically. "Much, much better."

The door at the end of the hall opens again and the innkeeper motions for me to come. The swarthy man picks up a shopping bag and walks down the hall. I pick up my backpack and follow, slowly, resigned to this weirdness, to another strange experience in a country full of them. A semi-crazed Brit in Delhi had told me, "India just doesn't stop," and I am starting to understand what he meant. I'm tired. It is the fact that pushes me forward. I will follow anyone promising a comfortable night's sleep.

I enter the room. It is large and well-furnished. It looks like it could be the drawing room to one of those mildewed and decrepit mansions that dot most of the cities here. The old man and his companion sit on fine leather chairs. The innkeeper, his head bobbing with great joy, points to an empty king-sized bed. On another bed sits the student, dressed in grey dress trousers and a white shirt. His hair is rumpled, his shirt creased. The look on his face indicates that he was either woken up abruptly or was caught masturbating. He manages a weak smile.

I sit on the empty bed and drop my backpack. "Drink?" the swarthy man asks.

"Yes!" the old man shouts. "Look at him! We all need drinks, but first we will require glasses!"

At this the innkeeper leaves the room. I look to the student, my roommate, and introduce myself. "I'm Ashok," he says wearily, shaking my hand.

"Our friend is ready to enter engineering school," the old man announces proudly. "I made his acquaintance this morning. Tomorrow we will take him to Mussorrie. It is beautiful and not so hot. The food is terrible and expensive. The scenery more than makes up for it, however. You should come as well."

"Mussoorie's not on my itinerary," I say. I haven't circled it in my *Lonely Planet*. The plan is to avoid the places tourists go, and Mussoorie is India's approximation of Banff. "I want to go north. To Dharamsala and Simla. Kulu and Manali. Try and get to Keylong." Keylong, everyone has been telling me, is a stunner, on the other side of the Himalayas, on the Tibetan Plateau.

"Fine, fine, you will have time for that later," the old man says. "But tomorrow we are spending the day in Mussoorie and you will join us."

The swarthy man pulls two bottles of Johnie Walker Red out of his shopping bag. He opens one and takes a swig and passes it to the old man who does the same. I'm not a Scotch drinker at all. I can't even remember if I've ever finished a glass of it.

The innkeeper returns with glasses and a funny smile on his face. He says something in Hindi. "Excellent!" the old man says, pointing a finger in the air.

The glasses are passed around and quickly filled. Triples, easily. The old man raises his glass. "A toast. To our American friend."

I put the drink to my lips and take a sip. My stomach makes a half-turn. My toes curl. But the taste that lingers on my tongue, the sweetness of it, is pleasing. My palate is a step ahead of my gut. I take another sip and my stomach turns a little more. I think I have heartburn. "I'm Canadian," I say breathlessly.

The old man stands bolt upright. "This is incredible!" he announces. "My son works at the Indian consulate in Toronto!"

The innkeeper claps. He obviously understands more English than he's let on.

"You must know him," the swarthy man says stupidly.

"I'm from Montreal," I say.

The old man sits again. "There's nothing wrong with that!" He takes a long sip of his drink. "My son posts the Scotch via diplomatic pouch. No tax. Very convenient. Drink up. Another toast!"

The swarthy man downs his Scotch in a dangerous-looking gulp. He's a professional, I think. The old man does the same. I've just realized that the innkeeper isn't drinking, and for whatever reason I find this annoying. Ashok takes the tiniest of sips. "Go on," the old man says to him, laughing. "This drink is civilization itself.

It's a pity what's happened to the Scots but there you go." Ashok closes his eyes and shoots the Scotch down and holds his head for a second. He stays like that, still, and then his eyes open and he is smiling triumphantly.

It is my turn. I'm still trying to figure out what happened to the Scots. And then I feel everyone's eyes on me, on the glass in my hand, and suddenly I'm a representative of Canada. This situation must be the definition of peer pressure. I stare at my glass, close my eyes and before I realize I've done it, the glass is empty, my insides on fire. Just as quickly, the fire subsides and I see myself holding my glass out for more. I may be drunk already.

A man wearing a dirty T-shirt and a *dhooti* enters, bearing an enormous platter of *tandoori* chicken. "Fabulous!" the old man says. The platter is placed on the floor and the lowly-looking man leaves.

"Eat, eat," the innkeeper says and he picks up the platter and holds it in front of me. I take a piece, reluctantly. I picture the scrawny dirt-eating chickens outside in the plaza. The smell is of spices and grilled protein and woodsmoke. The taste is otherwordly. Surely the chickens outside aren't the source of this.

The room is filled with the sounds of gluttony. The old man stands and raises his glass. "To Canada," he says. "It appears to be a nice place. At least in the photos I've seen."

He sits again, takes another gulp of his drink and leans toward me. He smiles, revealing teeth colored a macabre shade of yellow. "You have come a long way to visit us. We are honored. And what are you doing here, if one may ask?"

This is the question. It is one I can answer simply by saying, "Travelling" or "Visiting family," but it would not be remotely true. I don't tell him that I am here to find something. I don't tell him that I am here to escape a grievous disappointment back home. I don't tell him that I know only what I don't want to do with myself and that I think my future should be more than the end result of a process of elimination. I don't tell him any of this. I can't. I've just started to admit these things to myself. How can I possibly share them with strangers?

I down my Scotch and my stomach behaves. I have become acclimatized. I have come to India looking for answers to a question I am just starting to formulate—only to find that I enjoy Scotch. It's a start. I hold out my glass, and the swarthy man refills it. His hands leave grease marks all over the bottle. I take another piece of chicken. "I'm here to go to Mussoorie," I say.

 Arjun Basu was born and raised in Montreal. He was editor in chief of *enRoute* between 2001 and 2007. He continues to live in Montreal, with his wife and son, and his life is as squishy as anyone else's.